The Return

Don DeBon

The Return

Red Warp III

Don DeBon

First Printing
Copyright © 2020 Don DeBon

ISBN 978-1-948819-03-9
ISBN 978-1-948819-02-2 **(e-book)**

Contents

Chapter 1   3

Chapter 2   8

Chapter 3   12

Chapter 4   17

Chapter 5   23

Chapter 6   29

Chapter 7   41

Chapter 8   50

Chapter 9   56

Chapter 10   61

Chapter 11   78

Chapter 12   96

Chapter 13	105
Chapter 14	120
Chapter 15	127
Chapter 16	137
Chapter 17	148
Chapter 18	162
Chapter 19	173
Chapter 20	189
Chapter 21	210
Red Warp sample	229
Time Rock sample	241
Heart Of The Machine sample	250
About The Author	256

$$-1-$$

The mother of all rats ran across the floor and disappeared into yet another ragged hole in the wall as Trisia glanced up in disgust. She had tried to seal them, but there was always another. The place was a real dump. The sub-basement room was tiny, the power lines inadequate, and rat infested. Not to mention located in a part of town that made her worry about being mugged or worse every time she stepped outside. But it did have one advantage: it was cheap. And right now that was more important.

She turned a knob on her oscilloscope and the sine wave image on the monitor altered. It was almost enough. She pushed the setting beyond her Father's specs and the sine wave lined up, then faded a second later. She had built the device from her Father's notes, but it still refused to calibrate even after checking every component.

Trisia leaned forward, placing her elbows on the table and her head in her hands. So close, so very close. If only this quantum phase adjuster would pump out the proper frequency. Her thoughts paused as her head snapped up. "What if I couple the phase adjuster with the Professor's accumulator?" she muttered then shook her head. "No, that would take too long to build."

Equipment filled the room. She sat at the center, like a spider in the middle of an electronic web. In the one corner rested her power cell, duplicated exactly from the Professor's plans. But it had taken her almost a year to build and was far more expensive than she anticipated. She originally intended to use the normal power grid for her work, until she discovered the wiring in worse shape than the rest of the building. There was no way it could handle the current she needed.

The past year had given her many regrets. What she did to Professor Keleeigan especially. Upon learning of the true situation, he could have tried to help her Father before it was too late. Grief and rage convinced her to become one of the Professor's assistants and sabotage his time travel experiment. Never thinking he would want to share the moment with them instead of a private test drive. And later finding out the Professor had tried to warn her Father to the dangers of the cloaking device, but he refused to listen.

At first, she had discounted it. Why would her Father ignore the man that helped him with most of the groundwork? Now though, she realized it wasn't in the Professor's character to lie like that. It must have been the truth. She let out a deeply held breath. How Trisia wished she could go to him now for his help. But she knew the Professor would never help her now after almost stranding him in the ancient past.

Trisia tried again to bring the reluctant system in synchronic harmony with the rest of the equipment. It refused. Perhaps if she altered the power harmonic?

It might make the whole thing unstable, but she had to try.

To her surprise, it worked.

Trisia blinked. For there sat the monitor showing the perfect sine wave that had eluded her for many months. Before it could change again, she slammed her hand on the activation control.

The power cell's glow increased as energy flowed into the rest of the system, threatening to overload the very cables that sustained the whole network.

To Trisia's right, six dome shaped emitters sat equally apart around a vertical rectangular frame glowed to life. She adjusted another dial, and they increased in brightness, but nothing more.

"Come on! It has to work!"

She had spent every waking hour, every dollar she had of her inheritance on this project, and she was so close. But she was also almost out of time. The rent was due on this rat hole next week, and Mr. Wexler wouldn't take any more excuses. She would get evicted and all her equipment tossed out. With no other place to go, she couldn't let that happen.

Or be found.

The emitters glowed even brighter, and the frequency shifted. She tried to compensate but it refused, as if someone else was controlling it. The power cell glowed brighter and the power lines grew hot.

She reached for the emergency shutdown.

"Daughterrrrr," a voice groaned.

Trisia's eyes went wide, and she adjusted the emitters again. For the first time an angry green-black warp in space-time appeared in the center of the rectangle. It was working! It was finally working! "Hello?"

Trisia smelled the hot insulation and again reached for the shutdown.

The voice called again. "Daughterrrr. I knew you would come."

"Father?"

In the middle of the warp, a man-shaped silhouette appeared. "Who else?"

While Trisia always hoped for this moment, when she opened her mouth to speak, no words came out.

The figure came closer to the warp's threshold. "I always knew you could do it."

Trisia finally got her voice to work. "I knew you weren't dead! I knew Keleeigan had to be lying."

The figure took on a more defined shape, showing features on its face where before there were none. "Of course he was lying! Did you really think I would be wrong after all I proved was possible? I know you must have all of my research and notes, or we would not be talking now."

Trisia glanced over to at power lines. They were starting to glow white-hot. They couldn't last much longer. "Yes, I did get them. But the information was incomplete. I had to . . . improvise."

"Improvise? My data was perfect!"

Trisia shook her head. "No, it wasn't. There were gaps. I had to become Keleeigan's assistant to fill them in."

"You what!? After what he did to me? You helped him?"

Trisia shuddered. The memory of her Father's controlling nature when she was a kid came back in a torrent. "It was the only way. And I didn't do much other than get coffee."

"HA! Moris wouldn't have kept you around if you only made coffee. Even if you made him a cup, he would never get around to drinking it before mold appeared on the top!"

Trisia bit her lip. "Yes, you are right. But it was the only way."

Sparks flashed around the emitter assembly.

"We don't have much time. The system is failing."

"Fix it then."

"I don't know if I can. And even if I could, I don't have any money to make the attempt."

The figure smiled. "Daughter, do you think I wouldn't have provided for this?"

Trisia blinked. "What do you mean? I got the inheritance you left for me."

"Do you think I would leave everything so visible? I have assets far beyond what I left in my will. I never trusted lawyers not to take it all for themselves."

One of the emitters blew, and the warp rippled. Trisia boosted the energy in the rest, but she knew it wouldn't last more than a few seconds. "What do you mean?"

The figure's smile broadened. "Simple. Search for Ismov's Foundation. What you need is there." Another spark a second before all the emitters erupted in a blast of energy that knocked Trisia backward. A second later another wave from the phase adjuster mushroomed out, blowing every system one by one.

The lights above her popped, and the room went dark.

2

Trisia groped around in the dark, found a nearby flashlight, and flipped it on to survey the damage. Her nose wrinkled. The room stank of fried electronics and toasted wiring. All the emitters had blown, she knew that already, but so was the quantum phase adjuster and most of the electronics. Only the power cell had survived, and that was thanks to Professor Keleeigan's robust design, not hers.

Someone banged on her door. "Trisia? Are you okay? What happened? I thought I heard something exploding."

"I'm fine, Mr. Wexler. I just dropped a box of light blubs. Sorry I bothered you," she called out.

"Are you sure? Do I smell something burning?" the muffled voice responded.

"Yes. I'm sure. The smell is from something too close to the heater."

"Let me in and I will help you clean up."

"No need. The box was closed at the time, I just have to throw the whole box out. The other thing is fine."

"Very well, if you need me, you know where I am." Trisia heard diminishing footsteps and knew he had left. Mr. Wexler was a nice enough landlord, but rather nosy. She lost track of the times he had tried to make up some excuse to get inside.

While he still had a key, he would never use it unless there was an emergency. He wasn't a problem. It was the others in the neighborhood she wondered about.

Trisia shone her beam around the room and walked over to one light not connected to the rest. She plugged it into the wall and its dull orange light drove away the darkness. She blinked at the mess of now-useless equipment she had spent over a year accumulating.

Trisia sat in the room's only well padded chair in the corner and held her head in her hands. What was she going to do now? She had invested all she had, and then some, into this. And now it was all scrap, when she was so close. She had even proved her Father was alive! She had talked with him!

Her head shot up. *What was it he said? Check the Ismov Foundation?* She tried to think of all the different people her Father had worked with, no one named Ismov came to mind. Her head tilted to one side. *Wait a second, there was an old book my Father often carried with him called Foundation.* He once told her it was his lucky charm. She leapt from the chair and yanked out an old box from under one of the lab tables.

Trisia hadn't been able to keep much of her Father's stuff. Most of it she gave away except for his laptop, handwritten papers, and a few other items she had kept to remember him. She dug around in the box, pulling out two storage drives, and several file folders filled with loose papers. *There it is!* In the bottom laid a dirty, and well-worn copy of *Foundation* by Isaac Asimov. She pulled the book out and turned it over several times in her hands.

What did he want me to see? This is just an old novel. She flipped through the well-worn pages, but nothing stood out. No notes in the corner. Several pages were dog-eared but nothing else special about them. While she flipped through the book again her index finger touched a tiny bump along the back edge of the binding. She moved directly under the light and turned the book over several times, feeling the spine.

The bump didn't appear to be a manufacturing defect. Trisia ran her fingers over it again and the bump moved! Her eyes went wide as she pushed the bump to the bottom of the spine and a little data chip half the size of her fingernail fell out. She picked up the little chip, walked over to her Father's laptop that sat at the far end of the room, turned it on, and slid the tiny chip into a slot on the side.

At first nothing happened, then the backlight turned on causing the screen to flash several times. Trisia was glad she didn't have this laptop plugged into the monitoring equipment or it would have fried along with everything else. The screen flashed several more times before a blurry image appeared then resolved itself into the image of her Father.

"Trisia my daughter, if you are watching this it means I am dead, or worse. I have undertaken a mission that must be done, but there are risks. Very large risks. While I have taken every precaution and every test I know of says the system is now safe, Keleeigan's warnings still echo in my mind.

"For the moment, I will assume I am lost. While Keleeigan said the person would literally dissolve after prolonged exposure to the cloaking system, I know I have rectified that issue. However, it is still possible I may be lost in another dimension if the system's stability is affected in any way. Every test I have made says it is safe. But no simulated test is 100%. No doubt you have tried to find me and bring me back only to fail with the limited funds at your disposal.

"However, being that you have found this recording tells me you must have contacted me in some fashion, but require more assistance. I am here now to give you that assistance. When you inserted the chip into my laptop, not only was this recording activated but a secondary program as well. You will find all the funds you will ever need to bring me back, if it is possible, have been transferred from my hidden accounts to yours. I know you will make good use of them. And I want you to know, even if it fails, I have no doubts you did your best. The money will make sure you live out your life comfortably regardless if you succeed or not. It is the least I can do for my only daughter. I love you. Until we meet again."

The image winked out.

Trisia looked over to see faint traces of smoke still wafting from her laptop's ports and sighed. She tapped a few keys on her Father's and her financials came up causing her jaw to drop. She now had access to almost half a billion dollars. "How in the world did he get that much money?" she wondered aloud. She was about to shut down the laptop when another screen appeared with a map. It appeared to start on one end of the city's sewer system and went south. "What in the world is this?"

3

Professor Keleeigan peered through magnification goggles as he soldered another component to a circuit board. A gray hair drifted down, and he puffed it out of his vision. "This is taking a lot longer than I thought it would." The white lab coat draped across the back of his chair fell into the crook of the chair as he shifted, trying to ease his aching muscles.

James sat on the couch next to the worktable. He had finally traded in his standard FBI suit for a pair of shorts, polo, and black sneakers. Although, he still couldn't give up the jacket. He felt naked without it. Not to mention it concealed the energy pistol resting in the holster under his arm. The holster was once his Father's and had several features others lacked, including moving to hip or leg. Which is why he continued to use it, even though the bureau encouraged otherwise. And being custom-designed, it was more comfortable than most.

James turned towards Keleeigan causing the leather he sat on to squeak. Keleeigan's new lab didn't have many comforts. But then he was always too busy to use them. "Hmm? What was that Doc?"

Keleeigan looked up. "I said, this is taking a lot longer than I thought it would. I don't think it took me this long to build the system in the first place."

James smiled. "I doubt that. You are just impatient this time as you know it works."

"Perhaps. Still, I never would have thought it would have taken so long to get everything working again. Weeks maybe, but not over a month! Trisia really did a lot of damage."

James straightened as his head tilted down while keeping his eyes on Keleeigan. "She did? Or pushing the whole thing beyond its tolerances to get back here instead of being stuck in the past?"

Keleeigan let out a loud sigh. "You are right. But I certainly did not want to stay stuck in the Cretaceous period!"

James leaned back and laughed. "No, of course not. But you could have waited until Red and I could get there."

"My boy, if you remember, I tried. The dinosaurs had other ideas."

James laughed again. "True, and I know first-hand how hungry they are."

"Exactly. Also, I am putting in a few safeguards. The fluctuations of the temporal field last time almost ripped the whole space-time continuum apart. Even worse, I had no idea." Keleeigan went back to repairing the board. "You didn't need to stay here, you know."

James stood up, took several steps and placed his hand on the Keleeigan's shoulder. "I know. But with Trisia running around loose, we didn't think it was wise."

Keleeigan smiled but didn't look up. "What do you think she can do? She doesn't have much money, certainly not enough to rebuild my equipment. Even if she managed to download my designs, which I doubt."

James shrugged. "Maybe. But Red and I don't think it is worth the risk. Who knows what damage she could do.

Damage we might not be able to fix. At least not and be able to restore the time-line to as it was before."

"I agree my boy, I agree. If she had my designs. Naturally, she still doesn't have intimate knowledge of the system or how to get it running. Yes, she helped me build it, but I didn't share everything with her. You are the only one I have ever trusted 100%."

James smiled. "Thanks Doc."

"Don't mention it. You have more than earned it."

James looked around at the equipment and tables crammed into the basement that served as a makeshift lab. "Doc? I don't know why we didn't use your main lab."

"Because my boy, Trisia knows about that one. She doesn't know about my home. I want to keep her in the dark as much as possible. It gives us the advantage."

"But shouldn't we be there watching for her?"

Keleeigan laughed. "Hardly. I remote locked it down. No one can get in there but me now."

Atrus' hologram flashed on in front of Keleeigan, the artificial intelligence sported a big grin. "Oh, I bet I could."

"Well, anyone but you or me then. And we will know the instant anyone tries. Besides, you and Red deserve a little downtime." Keleeigan looked up. "Where is Red anyway?"

"Red is currently outside enjoying the back area and its liquid systems," Atrus said.

James smiled. "She does like your pool."

Keleeigan's attention went back to the circuit board as he soldered another component to it. "That she does. I'm surprised you are not up there with her instead of down here with this old man."

"I thought you might–"

"Need you? Other than helping me move everything here from the lighthouse, have I asked you to do anything else?"

"No."

"Take that as a hint. I know how you two feel about each other, so get out of here. Besides, if you don't want to be around Red in her swimsuit I need to check your pulse as you are obviously dead or close to it."

Atrus nodded. "I can confirm he is not dead. In fact, his pulse just shot up."

Keleeigan grinned. "Thinking of Red in her bikini no doubt."

Images flipped through his mind of Red in her various swimwear for several seconds before he snapped out of it and spoke. "Will you two cut it out! We–"

"We already know. And I'm sure Atrus knew long before I did. Now get out of here. Oh, and leave Atrus in case I need to bounce ideas off him."

James saw he wasn't going to get anywhere and sighed. "Sure Doc." He reached into his jacket and pulled a cylindrical device about the length of a pen but several times thicker from a pocket on the holster. He placed it on the table next to Keleeigan and headed up the stairs.

Doc's house was immense, though it should really be called a mansion. James made his way out back and found Red lounging by the pool. She was wearing a pink and black bikini that framed every curve. He felt his pulse race, and he forced it back. She could still drive him wild. He leaned over and kissed her cheek.

Her eyes snapped open. "Well, lookie who I see. Isn't it Mr. FBI agent? Hmm, I think so anyway, it has been a while since I have seen him."

He kissed her again. "Hey it hasn't been that long."

She smiled. "You forget, time is relative with me."

James sat down next to Red on the lounger. "I guess I'm in trouble then?"

Red grinned. "Well, that depends."

"On?"

She fluttered her eyes. "How fast you can get your suit on and join me."

"With an invitation like that, how can I refuse?" He leaned forward to kiss her again.

Atrus appeared next to them. "Atrus!" Red shrieked. "Don't do that!"

"My apologies, but we need you in the lab."

James hung his head and backed away from Red. "I left you with Doc, how are you here?"

"My holographic system does have a large range, but in this instance I tapped into Keleeigan's monitoring system and used one of the cameras to project through."

James blinked. "You can do that?"

"Certainly. It is a simple procedure. But again, you are both needed in the lab. Please. There has been a … unusual development."

Red blinked. "What happened?"

"It is best if I proceed in the lab."

James stood up. "We will be there in a minute."

"Very well." Atrus bowed and his image winked out.

"Talk about lousy timing," James grumbled.

Red slipped on her sandals and stood up. As she did, her lips met his. "It is, but I get a rain-check. Deal?"

James laughed. "Of course." He took her hand, and they headed for the lab.

— 4 —

Trisia swore as she saw another rat disappear into the darkness. She had been traipsing through the city's sewer system for what seemed like hours. Her feet were soaked, even though she wore boots, and the smell down here could stun a horse. But she was thankful it was in New York not some place she needed a passport to get to. She wasn't sure, but suspected Keleeigan had powerful friends that could block her from leaving the country. And leaving by clandestine methods would take too long.

Trisia turned another corner before checking the map. At least Mr. Wexler let her use his printer. She didn't want to risk bringing her Father's laptop down here and ruining it. That laptop was the only working electronic device she had left at the moment, not to mention she was certain her Father had more hidden surprises on its hard drive.

The map showed her destination lie past this section, then on the right. But when she got there, she sighed. No door, or anything special. Only a dead end recessed area. As she was about to leave, she turned back. *There must be something here. He wouldn't have led me down here for nothing.* She felt the various bricks, but they all appeared solid. She looked at the map again. Nothing about getting in. She was about to fold it up and put in her pocket when something caught her eye. In the corner of the map, written by hand were the letters LC3.

"LC3? What in the world could that mean?" Trisia cocked her head as she at looked the recessed bricks in more detail. "Could it mean a particular brick? Hmm, LC? Left corner?" She looked at the top of the recessed area and counted three bricks over, but it was too high for her to reach. Thinking of her Father, he wasn't tall either. There was no way he could have reached it. Her eyes fell to the bottom corner, and she counted three over.

The third brick felt loose, and after several tries she pushed it in. Trisia heard gears and the sound of a piston. Around the recessed area dust blew out of a crack now forming between it and the rest of the wall. It continued to recede into the wall, leaving a large walk-space to the right. She stepped inside, took two more steps along the walk-space before the piston started up again and pushed the brick wall back into place, sealing the entrance.

Trisia blew out a breath she didn't know she was holding and continued walking. If nothing else the smell was better in here, and she wasn't walking on God knows what. At the end of the walkway sat a large door with a keypad to the right. *Great, he didn't give me the code. Now what I am supposed to do?* The keypad's dull green screen called to her, and she decided on entering her birthday as a lark.

The keypad flashed "Incorrect access code. Activating secondary verification scan." Trisia froze as green lights reached out from the walls going up and down her body three times. "DNA verified. Welcome Trisia." The two-and-a-half meter tall door slid to the side, and she entered.

Trisia's mouth dropped for the second time in the past twenty-four hours, for the room was filled with the most advanced equipment she had ever seen. Heck, most of it she had never dreamed of, let alone what it might be used for. Rows upon rows of components in various stages of assembly. Every tool imaginable sat on the tables ready for use. Large computer clusters sat in the corners with their lights flashing, indicating they were processing something.

A large screen on the far wall lit up with her Father's smiling face. "Trisia my darling, I see you figured out my little riddle. Good. You will find this lab has everything you need. If it doesn't, you now have the means to acquire it. All of my research is here as well. Even more than the papers I am sure you were given to get this far.

"I have no doubt you can bring me back. I'm counting on you."

The image shrank to a point and disappeared. Trisia rolled up her sleeves, she had work to do.

Red and James made their way down the basement steps. "Doc? What is the problem?" James asked.

Keleeigan sat back in his lab chair. "I have found some rather disturbing data."

"What kind? I didn't think your equipment was functional yet."

Keleeigan shook his head. "It isn't. But during the rebuild I have boosted the sensitivity by using Red's crystal as a baseline. With this increase, I detected a space-time anomaly."

Red's eyes went wide. "You did? And you found a warp? Are you sure?"

"I did my dear. I still don't understand how exactly this crystal helps you," he paused to hand her a headband with a thin circular crystal with facets pointed towards the center mounted in it, "but I have used its properties to refine the delicate calibrations of my systems. And yes, I'm sure it is a warp. I wouldn't have sent Atrus after you otherwise. I confirmed with him"

Atrus appeared before them. "I have confirmed it is a warp, even if a highly unusual one."

"Highly unusual? That is bad. Very bad. We need to stop it immediately before it causes damage to the space-time continuum," Red said.

"Not quite that bad. It isn't a normal time warp. In fact, it was more of a dimensional warp with a very faint temporal signature."

Red cocked her head. "That doesn't make sense."

"I know."

James raised a finger. "Umm could you explain, for us lay folks what the heck is going on?"

Keleeigan smiled. "Certainly. Time warps you know about, it is what Red creates, and I created an inferior simulation. Although it worked quite well."

"Doc! What does this mean?"

"Sorry. Well, this warp is dimensional. Meaning the warp didn't travel in time, but only distance. Or rather the space between spaces."

James' eyes narrowed. "You mean another dimension?"

Keleeigan nodded. "Right. I detected it and Atrus verified. This warp didn't link to another time but a different dimension. I had a theory it was possible, but until now I never had the proof."

Red folded her arms across her chest. "But that makes little sense if it had a temporal signature."

Atrus smiled again. "It does if it happened in the future."

"You mean you picked up a warp that hasn't happened yet?" James asked.

"Right-o my boy. Interesting, isn't it?"

"Interesting? Interesting? This means Trisia did manage to steal your technology and is doing something with it. And that something can't be good. And you say it is interesting?"

Keleeigan laughed. "Well technically, she hasn't yet and won't for over a year. We have time to stop her before she does."

Red shook her head. "No, that is not possible. It would create one heck of a paradox. If we stop her before she does it, how would we know to stop her in the first place? Believe me, this is something we must *not* do. I had one experience in paradoxes and I will not do it again."

Keleeigan tilted back in his lab chair. "Oh, right. Should have thought of that," he mumbled.

James smiled. "Don't worry Doc, no one alive knows time travel better than Red. I knew, but only because I have been traveling with her for a while now."

Red started back up the stairs. "Where are you going?" James asked.

"To get changed. I am not time-traveling in this bikini."

"Why? We have over a year to prepare and find out what to do. And I'm sure Doc won't mind us hanging around."

Keleeigan smiled. "Nope, mi casa es su casa."

Red turned back and glared. "I'm not waiting a year. I will jump to her and find out what is going on. With or without you. I will not risk the whole space-time continuum by sitting around waiting for Trisia to make her move. She may not be traveling through time yet, but this proves she might at some point. We simply can't take the risk. And if she does create a temporal warp, and we find out now before the warp is created it will be too late to stop her without creating a paradox."

"But do we even know where to look?"

A holographic map appeared, and Atrus indicated an area in the center. "Yes. I have tracked her location to an area known as New York City."

James' eyebrows went up. "The city? How is that possible? Seems like someone would notice."

Keleeigan laughed. "Are you kidding? Most New Yorkers will ignore anything unless planes crash into buildings."

"In this instance the explanation is quite simple. The elevation indicates Trisia is deep underground," Atrus said.

Red resumed climbing the steps. "Not a problem. I can warp in on top of her if need be now that Atrus has the exact coordinates." The door closed behind her.

James watched the door close. "Guess we won't be using the rain check for quite a while."

"What was that?" Keleeigan asked.

"He means–" Atrus started to say.

"Atrus!"

"Yes, Mr. James?"

"Hush!"

"Acknowledged."

Wires stretched across the lab, linking one section to another. One table held a new and much larger phasing compensator, another held the power cell she had built. Emitters in a diamond outline were embedded into one wall and linked to the power cell. The smell of flux and fresh solder still hung in the air.

Trisia spent months on the new system. Even with all the money her Father had left, certain aspects weren't off the shelf and had to be built from scratch. The new phasing compensator being one. And this time she had installed safety systems between each section, which would blow before her valuable equipment did. A failure now wouldn't cause her to start again from the beginning.

She adjusted the compensator again. The sine wave fluctuated even still. Synchronicity had proven elusive. Still, this was the first night since she had rebuilt everything. Further calibrations were a given.

Trisia checked her new laptop and the server clusters. She had lost data in the last attempt, but not enough she couldn't try again once the settings were in proper alignment. She silently prayed it could happen tonight.

Trisia made one final adjustment and smiled at the perfect

sine wave now displayed. She activated the system, and the emitters began to glow brighter and brighter. She turned down the power a notch. While these emitters were far better than the old ones, she wasn't about to take chances on her first attempt.

In the middle of the emitters a small crack started to form. It started to grow then retracted. She adjusted the wave from .003% and it started to grow again centimeter by centimeter. At one point she lost patience and set the power level to full. The crack expanded to the full diamond outline of the emitters. The resulting warp fluctuated between a chaotic storm of green and red.

Trisia struggled to get the warp to stabilize. It flickered, flashed and threatened to implode in on itself. She reduced the power to the emitters, and to her surprise, it worked. The warp stood there displaying a churning mass of green and black, but stable.

"Daughter ... I knew you could do it."

Trisia looked closer into the warp and saw nothing. Then a vague silhouette of a man appeared in the distance. It approached quickly and the featureless face smiled. "Hello?"

"Is that all you have to say to your long-lost Father?"

Trisia blinked. While she always hoped this would work, she still had doubts it would so quickly. "Dad?"

"Of course. Who else could have guided you to find me? Now initialize the sub system I set up, so I may leave this prison of a dimension."

"I ... I don't know how."

"You have access to my systems in the lab. Search the cluster for a program called IDT-return."

"I don't understand."

"You know about the cloaking system or you would not

be here now. While Keleeigan was correct in his assessment, I made modifications to the original design. I thought I had anticipated every possible fault, but I knew there was a chance I could have missed something. Hence the plan you are now executing."

Trisia blinked. "The plan?"

The shadow in the warp shifted its position several times, showing obvious annoyance. "We are wasting time!" Linus Sanford growled. "Very well, I suppose you should know. I added another phasing component to the cloak, allowing for a dimensional shift more than infrared. Though I couldn't get rid of it totally without being lost in the other dimension. And it worked. But something went wrong. I am not sure what as I thought I had every conceivable failure anticipated.

"However, you know me. I always have a backup plan. You are that backup plan. You and this lab. When you activate the IDT program, it should lock on to me and allow me to return."

"One thing I do not understand, why did you try to assassinate our president in the first place? What you told me before doesn't add up."

The shadowy form shifted as if stung. "I am sorry about that. It was not something I wanted to do. In fact, I wasn't planning on hurting him. Only making it look like I did."

Trisia folded her arms over her chest. "Explain."

"I needed funding. The only one interested in my idea is another large ... um ... country. At least the only one that had enough funding to back up their offer. But once I created the prototype, I fully intended to take everything back to our own country. However, they found out about my true loyalty and forced me to show them proof I would not do what they suspected."

"They told you to assassinate our president?"

Linus' head bobbed up and down. "Yes, they never liked the guy and to be honest neither did I. Still, I wasn't about to kill someone for them. Let alone our president! I thought about trying to disappear, but these people had ways of finding me. Even worse, they knew where you were and threatened to take action against you if I didn't fulfill their request.

"I felt trapped, but I figured out a solution. They had supplied me with a special gun and ricin pellets to kill without letting the target know until I was far away. I removed the ricin pellets and made my own with my own special mix of an agent giving the simulation of ricin poisoning, but not be fatal. I figured this would buy me enough time to find you before we both disappeared. Even after I was discovered, I had to make it look like I was a crazed assassin, for both our sakes."

Trisia bit her lip. "But they found out?"

Linus nodded. "Yes. But I didn't know it until after my ...accident."

"Wait. How did you find out then?"

Linus waived the shadowy form of a pistol in his hand. "I still have this. Being alone in your own dimension, well it was one thing I could look at besides myself."

"How did the pistol tell you they had found out?"

Linus blew out a breath, which made Trisia wonder what he was breathing. From what she knew, nothing existed where he was. Or even how he was surviving in the first place. "I had carefully labeled the pellet loader. While the cartridge here is empty and looks like the one I labeled, the indicator is off a millimeter. Meaning, they had switched my labels, and I was firing ricin pellets instead of my own! The change was so slight, I didn't notice it until I was floating around in here with nothing else to do. You must believe me, it was not my intent. And I didn't want to lie to you earlier, but they might have been monitoring my communications. And if I encrypted them, they would have become even more suspicious."

Trisia nodded. "I do. But one thing still puzzles me. I can see you. Why don't you step through the warp?"

Linus shook his head. "It doesn't work that way. I don't have enough energy here to push myself through. Hence I need you to pull."

Trisia nodded. "I understand," she tapped a few keys on her laptop, "I have engaged the program." The power cell began to glow brighter and brighter as the more power was drawn from it. The emitters also increased in brightness. Sparks flared from one of them and the shadow shivered.

"Dad! I have to abort!"

"Not yet!"

Another spark from one emitter and the shadowy figure of Linus Sanford faded slightly. "Turn it off!"

"I'm trying!" Several of the emitters sparked this time and figure faded further before she could get the system to terminate.

Linus' head bobbed around amongst the green and black clouds surrounding him. "That was close. I was being dissolved instead of brought through."

"I think I have found out why. The clusters didn't have enough computational power to lock on to you. Your form is in constant flux and moving. It is too much for them to pull you through."

"Get more clusters then! Fill the room with them! I provided you with the resources!"

"I know, but from what I can tell here. It still wouldn't be enough. We need beyond what a thousand of them could do."

Linus hung his head. "Then I am lost. I won't be able to stay here forever. I could feel myself fading even before the attempt."

"Maybe not. I know of something beyond what is possible in our current level of technology."

Linus cocked his head. "How–"

"Never mind. Let's say Keleeigan has met some very interesting friends since you saw him last. One of these friends can help us. And from what I have seen. I suspect they are on their way even now."

— 6 —

Red stood stretching in Keleeigan's spacious back yard wearing her skin-tight bodysuit. James walked closer, shouldering his backpack. He had exchanged the shorts and shirt for his usual uniform consisting of black pants, dress shirt, and tie. "Are you sure about this? I still think we should wait and let Doc examine the data before we run headlong into this. Whatever this is."

Atrus flashed on in front of them. "Not to mention me. I would like further time to examine the data."

Red rolled her eyes. "Listen you two, we don't have time. I explained this earlier. If something else changes, we may not be able to correct it, or jump without creating a paradox. We *can't* wait."

James' stance shifted and he sighed. "You're right, of course. But I still think we have a little time, perhaps not a year. But at least a few days."

Red walked up and stuck her finger in his face. "After all this time with me and you still are not thinking in the 4th dimension. Time is relative, forget a year or even a week. We may not have three seconds. That means we jump *now,* not a second later. Got it?"

James raised his hands in front of him in a spreading motion back and forth. "Okay okay, I give. It is my turn to have a bad feeling is all."

Red nodded, taking several steps back. "Noted. Now ready yourselves, we are jumping."

"I just hope the coordinates are right."

Atrus nodded. "They are. The location I have given is two meters south of the warp we detected. Given what we know of warps, it should be an open space and easy to land."

"We hope," James said.

"I should be able to tell before we exit if there is a problem," Red said. She lowered herself into a sprinting position, a microsecond later began running faster and faster in a clockwise direction. James took several large steps to the right out of the center as he knew what was coming.

The air began to swirl as dust and dirt were lifted and carried along in Red's wake. She increased her speed, causing leaves and branches to detach and follow her in the maelstrom. A storm of her own making. Atrus disappeared rather than try to maintain his image inside the storm, which was proving difficult. Clouds rolled in and a second later lighting struck the earth dead center. A crack opened in the very fabric of space and time. A crack James knew would grow.

Red increased her speed again and the crack widened several times into a warp. James looked into the chaotic mass of red and black energy the warp consisted of. "Ready?" James shouted.

"Not yet ... almost!" Red shouted back. She performed another burst of speed and the warp flickered. "Now!"

James ran for the center and jumped in with Red following a microsecond later. The warp slammed shut with a thunderous crack and the storm died, dropping the bones of trees as it did.

Keleeigan looked out from his patio doors and sighed. "God speed you two, I hope you aren't running into a trap."

Red and James floated inside the warp. James kept his eyes shut lest he lose his lunch. He was thinking this should be a short trip when he felt himself being engulfed by an exit point.

Inside the lab, lighting flashed as a warp opened. James crashed out and rolled to the side with Red landing a second later. The warp slammed shut with a loud boom. They got to their feet and looked around. James blinked several times to make sure, but they were inside a metal structure consisting of interconnected metal squares. "What the heck? A cage?"

Red pulled at a hinged part of the metal that appeared to be a door, but it held fast. "Would seem so."

"Well, you can open it right?"

Red nodded. "Given time. It is too soon after creating the warp. Even with such a quick trip, I have to replenish my energy."

"I told you this was a bad idea."

"Oh, shut it."

"Well, I guess it is up to me then." He reached into his jacket for the energy pistol Keleeigan had designed.

From the corner a woman stepped out from behind a large computer cluster. "Welcome to my lab. I have been expecting you."

"Trisia," James said through gritted teeth, his fingers curled around the weapon hidden under his jacket, "what are you doing? Let us out this instant."

"What am I doing? I thought it would be obvious. Capturing you."

Red's eyes narrowed. "I don't know what you are planning but we will stop you."

"Stop me? I doubt it. Heck, you are going to help me."

Red laughed. "Help you? Never. Because of you, Keleeigan was almost lost in the distant past. Not to mention the resulting instability from his malfunctioning equipment would have destroyed the entire space-time continuum if we hadn't stopped it."

Trisia nodded. "All true. Which is why I knew you would come here. You couldn't resist the beacon I sent. Accidental at the time, but in the end very beneficial. And the portable Faraday cage makes a good temporary holding cell, don't you think? Of course, I had to bolt it down so you can't slide your way out."

James sighed, removing his hand from his jacket. Safe in the knowledge he could still use the weapon if needed. "I told you this was a trap."

"Quite right. I knew you would be on your way once Atrus or Keleeigan noticed the disturbance."

"I told you," James said out the corner of his mouth.

Red glared. "Will you shut it! Now is not the time." She turned her gaze back to Trisia. "Whatever you want, you will not get it."

"What I want is very simple: to free my Father."

James blinked. "Free him from what? He's dead."

"Au contraire. He is alive. Trapped in another dimension. I know you didn't try as the Professor said he dissolved into nothingness. And if my Father had used the exact same system Keleeigan and he designed, then he would have. But he didn't. The modifications allowed him to live, but trapped in another dimension. Now I want to free him."

Red's eyes narrowed. "You might be able to sell this story to others, but not me. What is it you really want?"

"Fine. You want proof. I'll give you proof." Trisia walked over to her laptop and tapped a few keys. The lights flickered as the power cell glowed to life and grew in intensity. "Turn around and watch."

Behind the cage, the dome emitters set into the wall glowed bright orange. A second later the green warp appeared.

"I've never seen a warp like that," James whispered out of the corner of his mouth.

"Neither have I," Red whispered back.

"Oh, it gets better. Father, show them," Trisia said.

Red and James watched as a shadowy form appeared in the distance and came closer. The face smiled. "Nice to meet you. Now help me leave this prison."

Both their eyes widened but Red's narrowed as she spoke. "There is no way I am going to help you. I came back to stop the assassination of a president which caused a great temporal event. As far as I am concerned, you got what you deserved."

Trisia approached them and pointed to the warp. "He only did it because he was forced to. And his original plan was to make the President appear dead to buy time so we could both disappear. His financial partners didn't tell him what they were planning until it was too late. Then double crossed him by learning of his subterfuge and tricking him into using the real ricin pellets. It was not his fault. He was trying to save me!"

James cocked his head as he leaned against the cage. "How

can you believe that? It is a story he made to get you to help him. Doc said the cloak would cause mental instabilities."

"Yes, if he used the original design. Which he didn't."

Red turned. "Is it possible Keleeigan was wrong?"

James laughed. "Ha! Don't tell me you are falling for this?"

"I'm not falling for anything," she paused the point at the shifting green mass in front of them, "that warp is different from any others I have ever seen. I suppose it is possible."

"I still don't buy it. If we can see him, it seems like you could save him yourself."

"I don't have the energy to push myself through. As I have told her, she needs to pull. We already tried it, and I almost faded from existence," the figure said.

Red crossed her arms. "I don't know what you need us for then. I don't have any power source. Neither does James, except for his gun, and it has far less than the power cell you have sitting on the table over there."

"I don't need your energy, I need your computational power."

Red blinked. "You want Atrus?"

"Yes. The arrays I have aren't powerful enough. While I could get more, even if I filled this room, they still wouldn't be enough. But I think he could do it," Trisia said.

"Who said we brought him?" James said with a smirk.

"I am not falling for that, just like you didn't believe my story. You always carry him. I can't imagine you not bringing him."

Atrus appeared inside the cage with Red and James. "Very astute of you."

"Atrus! What are you doing? I told you to remain hidden unless we called," James said.

"Sir, if I can save a human's life with no risk to you or anyone else, nor cause temporal damage. I will do so."

Trisia smiled. "Smart. Now give him to me so I can link him to the system."

"No need. I have linked to your system, and I have located the program you used in your earlier attempt to retrieve Mr. Sanford. I see several errors in its design and I have corrected them. I have a lock. Initiating the retrieval."

The shadowy figure flashed several times as he was pulled towards the warp. He cried out in agony as he reached the edge of the warp and began moving through it.

"Stop! You are killing him!" Trisia shouted.

"It is proving more difficult than I anticipated. Correcting calculations and increasing power level," Atrus said.

A hand emerged from the green horizon of the warp followed by an arm. Then a shoed foot broke through the edge of the vortex.

Trisia reached for the hand and grabbed it. "Come on Father, you can do it!" She pulled. A second later Linus Sanford fell out of the warp and on top of Trisia.

Atrus shut the system down and the warp slammed shut.

Linus got to his feet, a little wobbly at first but soon passed. "Thank you."

Trisia jumped up and grabbed Linus in a strong hug. "Father! It is so good to have you back!"

"It is good to be back. And now I am sorry for what I must do." He looked towards the ceiling. "System command 3423 target all females." Red beams shot out of every corner of the room and centered on the women's foreheads.

Trisia blinked as her eyes drifted up. "Father? I don't understand. What are you doing?"

"Getting power my darling Daughter. The ultimate power.

The control of time itself. I was quite happy to settle for the dimensional transportation you have now helped me to perfect, but when you mentioned what Red can do, it is an opportunity I cannot pass up."

Red glared. "I won't help you."

"I didn't expect you would, my dear." Linus noticed James reaching for his weapon. He pointed. "I wouldn't do that if I were you. The system is also set to take action if a weapon is shown."

James stopped with his hand under his jacket. "Anymore bright ideas?" James grunted.

"Sure. Atrus take care of this."

"I regret to inform you I cannot. When this security system activated, it restricted my access. I am attempting to regain full control, however, an encryption system I have not seen before is now in place. It will take me a few minutes."

Linus grinned. "Time you do not have. Now I want you to upload all data you have accumulated while inside the warps to my server cluster."

Atrus shook his head. "No. Such data is too dangerous."

"Then both of these women will die."

"Father! Please! If it wasn't for me, you would have been trapped there forever!"

"Silence!" Linus looked at James. "You have a minute to comply or these women die."

James hung his head. "Atrus, do it."

"What?" Red exclaimed.

"I don't see another way out, do you? And I am not going to let you die. Besides, he will not be able to do anything with the data. He is not you or Doc."

"Perhaps not, but it's not worth this risk."

"Saving your life is! Atrus, do as I said."

"Very well." Atrus' hologram turned towards the server cluster. "Data has been uploaded."

Linus went over to Trisia's laptop and hit several keys. "Excellent! Thank you. It is now time I bid you all adieu." He activated the system and another green warp appeared in the middle of the emitters.

"Father? What are you doing?"

"Saying goodbye." He leaned forward and kissed Trisia on the cheek. "Thank you my Daughter, I will always be grateful." He jumped into the warp and disappeared. A second later the warp sealed itself with a loud crack.

James leaned against the metal grid. "Anyone have any other bright ideas?"

Lights all over the lab began flashing red. "Warning core system coolant has been suspended. System will overload in one minute," a voice boomed.

"Great, just when you didn't think things could get any worse. Atrus, how goes the hacking?"

"Very well. But I will not finish in the time left to us."

"I have an idea. Atrus, use your holographic system to make me appear as a man," Red said.

"What for? How is that going to help?" James asked.

"Easy, Linus instructed the system to target all females. I'm betting it will forget all about me if I appear as a man."

Atrus nodded. "I will do so, but I must remind you if your movements are too quick, I will not be able to keep up the simulation around you and this system may take action."

"Understood." Trisia blinked as Red's features melted away, reappearing as a bald man in his thirties wearing a blue jeans and a t-shirt. Red looked down. "Good job Atrus." She walked over to the door of the cage and placed her hand on the lock. A second later a slight click could be heard, and she opened the door. She looked back at James. "Well, come on. Or do you want to stay here while this place blows?"

James smiled. "You didn't need to ask."

Trisia blinked. "What about me?"

"I say we leave her," James said.

Red glared. "She was tricked as much as we were. Atrus, one hologram disguise please."

"Certainly. But I need to scan her first."

"Warning! System is now critical and will fail in thirty seconds," a voice boomed.

James reached into his holster and pulled out Atrus. "What a time to need a scan." He held him out and a green beam shot from the tip. The horizontal ray went up and down Trisia several times before retracting.

"Done. Initiating holographic disguise around Trisia." A second later Trisia looked down at her flat chest. A millisecond after, the red beams on her forehead disappeared.

"Wow, this is wild." Trisia pointed to a door on the opposite wall. "Come on, this way." They moved as fast as the holographic cover would let them. When they reached the door, she touched the keypad, it recognized her and the door slid open.

Behind them sparks erupted from one of the computer cores, spreading quickly to every core in the room. They dove through the door as Trisia slapped the control to seal it. Flames erupted through the crack before it could close all the way.

Red and Trisia's disguises shimmered away as James sat leaning up against the smooth cold wall. "Whew, that was close."

"Too close." Trisia said as she got to her feet, thankful the lab didn't have a direct exit to the sewer system. The mere idea of landing in a pile of feces and rats turned her stomach. She turned around and tried to open the door again, but it refused. The access keypad still glowed, but wouldn't acknowledge her. "Darn, the door's circuitry must have fried."

James stood up and pulled the energy pistol from its holster under his arm. "Let me handle this." He popped open the control panel hidden in the grip, adjusted several settings, and closed the grip. He aimed and fired. A blast of energy erupted from the barrel and slammed into the door. For a second nothing appeared to happen. Then the door's molecules broke down and dissolved, leaving an open doorway.

"That must be handy if you forget your keys," Trisia said.

"Yeah, but Red isn't too happy if I leave atomized doors around all the time."

"And you like to do it too often," Red said.

James looked back over his shoulder as they walked back inside the lab. "I didn't know you were counting."

The fumes of fried electronics and melted equipment almost made them double over. Dust, debris, and black soot covered everything. The tables and their contents were either burnt or melted into a puddle. The emitters sagged, half-melted. Every core was either a liquified pile of plastic and electronics or were missing entirely.

James looked around, blinking fast. His eyes stung and he wiped them with his sleeve. "Looks like everything here is toast."

Trisia ran over to a table containing a black, half-melted rectangle. "Even my laptop! I'm going to kill him! This is the second one I've lost this year!"

"Grab it and we can call Keleeigan to come and pick us up. Perhaps we can recover something."

Atrus appeared in front of them. "I have taken the liberty of doing so. He will arrive in twenty minutes."

7

Red, James, and Trisia stood on the open street as Keleeigan's car hovered down in front of them and Trisia stared at it open-mouthed. While she thought she had seen it once before out of the corner of her eye, she was never positive. James smiled. "Yeah, he figured out how to make cars fly."

Trisia blinked. "How?"

"I didn't ask. I'm not exactly a scientist or inventor."

"I can tell you, if you have several days available," Atrus said.

"Not now, Atrus," James said as he opened the door. "Hi Doc, thanks for the pickup."

Keleeigan shifted in his seat and adjusted several controls. "No problem my boy, been expecting your call."

"How?"

"I will fill you in later. But for now, let's say I had a year to enhance my tracking system." He turned his head and his eyes met Trisia's. "What's *she* doing here?"

"Long story Doc, and we need to get going," James said as he climbed into the car. Red sat in the back seat but Trisia stood on the sidewalk not sure what to do.

"I'm sure, but this vehicle is not moving until I get some answers."

"Maybe it is best if you go on without me. I'll be fine," Trisia said.

James reached out and grabbed her hand. "No way, Linus isn't stable and we can't risk he will try to use you again. We already know he can."

Keleeigan grabbed James' shoulder. "Wait! Linus? What are you talking about? He's dead."

James licked his lips as his head turned. "Umm Doc, that is one of the things we need to talk about. No, he isn't and he is back."

"That's not possible!"

Atrus flashed into existence sitting next to Red. "I assure you Professor Keleeigan, it is, and he has."

James glanced back at Keleeigan. "Look, she was tricked as much as we were. Linus even tried to kill her. All she was trying to do was save him, and as a thank-you he tried to kill her and us!"

"Well, why didn't you say so in the first place." He motioned to the back seat. "Get in, we don't have a second to lose."

Trisia sucked in her bottom lip. "Umm, it is taken." Everyone in the car looked at Atrus.

"What is the problem? She can still sit here. I am only a hologram." They glared and Atrus rolled his eyes. "Very well, if you insist." His imaged winked out and Trisia sat in his place. Keleeigan gunned the engine, and they took off into the sky.

A short time later they were in Keleeigan's basement lab. New equipment and several more tables crowded the space. "I see you have been busy Doc," James said.

"I told you I was. I have enhanced the system I used to first detect the warp you both went after. Another warp appeared less than an hour ago. However, while it had an unusual shift like before, it lacked the temporal signature. If I hadn't increased the dimensional sensitivity, I never would have seen it. And while the shift itself was much stronger than before, the lacking temporal signature made it a lot harder to track. I figured this had to be Trisia again and awaited your call."

Trisia shook her head. "It wasn't me that time. It was my Father."

Keleeigan sat back in his lab chair and folded his arms. "I think you had better fill me in."

Trisia sighed as she looked at Red and James. They both nodded and she began. "First, I want to say I am sorry for deceiving you. I was blinded by the information my Father had given me, labeling you as the reason for his loss. I managed to download some of your work, including the plans for the power cell."

Keleeigan sprang forward. "You what!"

Red held up a hand. "Professor, please let her finish."

Keleeigan leaned back and rotated his chair back and forth. "I'm listening."

"Other than the power cell, I didn't get much else. But it was enough, when coupled with my Father's notes, to build a possible doorway to where he was trapped."

"And how did you know he was there and not dissolved into nothingness as I told you?" Keleeigan asked.

Trisia sat down on the couch along the wall opposite Keleeigan. "From one of his more obscure notes. After I *left*, I dug deeper and found some vague information about the modifications he made to the cloaking system. It wasn't quite the system you both had originally envisioned. It still pushed the user out of the normal visual spectrum, but it did so with a dimensional curve. This–"

"A dimensional curve? Are you kidding? He is better than I gave him credit for."

"Yes. While it worked, something went wrong as you know. Based on what I could ascertain from his notes, I theorized he could be trapped in another dimension. Perhaps the power source he was using failed, or it didn't close all the way sucking him inside. I don't know. But I figured I had to try.

"Being he had disappeared for almost two years, I got him declared dead–with the assistance of his previous coworkers– I received his effects, including a lot more of his research notes. With the small inheritance he left, I built a power cell like yours, although of lesser capacity. The problem was the expense. I didn't plan very well and I ended up in a rat hole basement room for a lab.

"I did manage to contact him there though for a few seconds. But it was long enough for him to pass a cryptic message leading me to more funds and a secret lab he had built deep in the city sewers. With the new lab and the added resources, I tried again. This time I could reach him, but failed to pull him through. His form was in constant flux and the computational cores I had weren't enough. Heck, a football field full of them wouldn't be enough."

Keleeigan made a sour expression. "And you thought of Atrus."

Trisia nodded. "I knew he would have the processing power to lock on to my Father with ease. And he did. What I didn't expect was my Father casting me aside afterward like a dirty piece of tape."

"My dear, you have nothing to be ashamed of. Well, other than stealing from me. You didn't need to you know. If you had explained the situation, I would have helped. I assume sabotaging of my lighthouse was to cover your theft?"

Trisia's head lowered as she nodded.

"To be honest, I have felt guilty regarding Linus' disappearance. I always wondered if there was something I could have done. But everything I had said no. I would be very interested in the papers you inherited."

"I doubt you would be now. Unless you can read charcoal," Red said.

Keleeigan cocked his head. "I don't understand."

Trisia sighed. "There is more. After I freed my Father from his dimensional prison, he turned on me. He used a voice command I wasn't aware of to lock the lab's defenses on Red and myself. He threatened to kill us unless Atrus gave my Father his data recorded during Red's travels."

"You didn't give it to him, did you?"

"Not at first," Red said.

Keleeigan's eyes went wide. "But you did?"

"He didn't give us much choice. And we didn't think he could use the data anyway," James said leaning against the wall.

"That was idiotic. I figured it out and I didn't have in-depth data recordings from *inside!*"

Atrus flashed on in front of Keleeigan. "I tried to tell them of the possibility. But they were adamant I upload the data. However, no instruction was given on how accurate the data had to be."

Keleeigan smiled. "You sly ol' dog. How much variance did you insert?"

Atrus cocked his head. "I assure you I am not a dog. The variance is point-five enough to throw off stability by a large margin, yet make the data appear accurate."

Keleeigan rubbed his chin. "That gives us the advantage. He may or may not figure that out. Are you sure nothing remains of his notes? Perhaps on the sad-looking laptop Trisia is holding?"

Red pointed to the rectangular mass of melted plastic sitting on Trisia's lap. "I told her to bring it. I thought perhaps you might get something off of it."

Trisia handed it over to Keleeigan, and Atrus moved to the side. "I will take a look. It might be like an oyster with a pearl within. Once I peel it apart that is."

"There is no need. I have scanned the device in question. The primitive magnetic storage device's metal platters have melted. Data is irrecoverable," Atrus said.

"Blast it. I needed to see those papers."

Trisia smiled. "I never said it was the only copy." They all turned and looked at her. "I had my laptop set on a remote backup service. All the data he had is there." She walked over to an unpowered computer sitting to Keleeigan's left. She pointed. "May I?" Keleeigan nodded, and she powered it up then logged into the remote system. "There you are. That is the folder containing all the scans of his papers and other files."

Keleeigan leaned over and examined the images. He zoomed in on several diagrams. Some of it he recognized from back when they were colleagues, but other sections were like nothing he saw before. After ten minutes of study, he turned away from the screen. "From what I can see here, the dimensional shift he created is quite ingenious. But I still see it creating the same mental instabilities I warned him about. It is safer, yes, but not enough I would risk using the device."

James pushed himself off of the wall. "Doc, what about a warp that looks very different from Red's? Say predominately green? It is what Linus created and went through."

"I have no idea. I am not an expert on warps. Red knows more about them than I do."

Red shook her head. "Not really. I am not sure how I do what I do."

"Hmm I wonder. Trisia? What did Linus use before he left?"

"Why, my laptop."

Keleeigan pointed. "This one?" She nodded. "And was the auto backup still on at the time?"

She shrugged. "It should have been."

"Doc? What are you thinking?"

"Hang on a sec, let me look." Keleeigan scrolled through the updates searching for the most recent changes log. At the very end he found several commands and data downloaded from elsewhere. "Ahh, here we go. Well I'll be, he used his method, with a few additions, to create a dimensional door. Not sure where he got the rest of this data, perhaps from being in the warp itself trapped between dimensions. Either way, he made it work."

Red cocked her head. "A dimensional door?"

"Or a warp that folds space from one location to another. Essentially a door or gateway from one location to another. Instantaneous travel to any point, provided you have the power and coordinates available. From what I can see, he figured out a way to fold space using the other dimension he was in as a medium between the two. So you walk through one side in one location and end up in another on the other. To the traveler it would look like one simple step through. When you are actually traveling between dimensions to do it."

James blinked. "Red can travel from one location to another and stay in the same time-zone. But her warps look a lot different. Are these warps Linus made safe?"

"It would depend on your definition of safe. They are stable and aren't going to destroy the space-time continuum. While it is hard to tell the exact details from this, I can determine the cloak holds you suspended between dimensions while still trying to keep you here but out enough so no one sees you. Yet still leaves you able to still interact with the physical universe. The straddling between dimensions is the danger. That much constant interdimensional stress will cause havoc with the neurons in your brain. Other cells too, but at a much slower pace. The body could regenerate that aspect. But the brain damage is more permanent."

"He didn't seem any different," Trisia said.

Red choked. "What do you mean? He tried to kill us! Are you saying he has tried to kill you before and it was normal?"

"No, I mean he didn't look …I don't know what I mean. Okay you are right, he is insane," Trisia said with a sigh.

"I have found the coordinates Mr. Sanford used," Atrus said.

"How? I thought you didn't have that kind of access after he enabled the security system?" James said.

"Correct. However, since Sanford used Trisia's laptop to enter those coordinates, and she had the data backup system in place, we have a log of the last activity he did. It would also appear he transmitted all the data I gave him, along with contents of the cluster."

Red leaned forward. "The same location?"

Atrus shrugged. "Possible. I cannot make such a determination based on what I have available."

"I bet he has another lab stashed there." Red looked over to James. "Are you ready for another jump?"

James smiled. "I was going to ask you the same thing. You do all the work, I just ride along."

Keleeigan raised his hand. "Now wait a second. You don't know what you are jumping into. It could be another trap. He is certain to know you are coming."

"I doubt it. As far as he knows, he locked Atrus out of his systems. And he doesn't know about Trisia's little cloud backup service. That gives us the advantage. And we are talking about someone that might be able to warp to any location on the planet. Not to mention if he is able to figure out temporal warps from Atrus' data. I can't risk waiting," Red said.

Keleeigan sighed and stood up, stuffing his hands into the pockets of his white lab coat. "While I agree you need to go after him. I don't think you have to this instant. He has been away for almost two years. If he has gone to another lab, he will still have a lot of work to do before warp creating is possible. I think we need to approach this with careful planning. Besides, Atrus and I can detect any warps he tries to create, now that we know how he is doing it."

Atrus nodded. "I am scanning now, and will continue to do so. The instant one is detected, we will know the location."

8

Electrical discharges shot out from the center of the alleyway. A bubble rippled out and a flashing green warp appeared in its wake. A second later Linus Sanford crashed out onto the pavement. The warp folded in on itself and disappeared.

Linus stood up and looked around. No one in the area. *Good, I won't have to kill anyone.* A cool wind hit him and he stuffed his hands into the pockets of his pants and walked out of the alleyway. The smell of the nearby Chinese restaurant hit him first as he exited. Looking left and right, he turned and headed for it.

Inside, the customers were sparse at this time of night. He walked up to the counter and ordered several egg rolls.

"Will that be here or to go?" the young Asian girl behind the counter asked.

"To go. Oh, and throw in a few cookies as well."

The girl nodded, and a minute later brought him an oyster pail. Linus reached into his back pocket and his eyes went wide. He forgot he left his wallet with all of his other ID before the last mission and was subsequently lost. "I . . . umm seem to have lost my wallet. I don't understand I had it–"

The girl smiled as she turned to look towards the kitchen. She leaned forward and lowered her voice. "If you won't tell my boss, I won't either. They are several hours old and I would have had to throw them out anyway." She pushed the pail towards Linus.

He leaned forward and whispered, "Thank you." Grabbed the pail and slipped it under his arm. He left the restaurant and made his way to an old building on the very edge of town.

Munching on an egg roll, he approached a dilapidated building that appeared condemned. But Linus knew better. He walked passed the various danger signs and headed for an elevator in the back. Glass shards crunched under his feet from numerous broken windows and the place still smelled of being burnt to a crisp. He reached the elevator. It sat dead and motionless with the keypad to its right blank and unlit. He flipped a hidden switch under the controls and it lit up. *Good, they haven't detected the power tap yet.* Linus entered a code and the elevator groaned to life with the doors grinding their way open a minute later. He entered and punched in another code on the corresponding keypad. The doors shut with a squeal and elevator began to descend.

A minute later the elevator opened to the subbasement, and Linus smiled. Tables sat full of components. Boxes and boxes of stored materials sat stacked in a makeshift storage room. The computer cores sat in every corner of the room, their lights still glowing, indicating their readiness. The lab was as he left it.

Linus walked over to one of the control stations, sat his open oyster pail down on the table and plopped into the padded desk chair next to it. Leaning forward, he tapped several keys as he checked the cores. Another smile crept across his face, they had received his transmission earlier. All the data from the small lab and his Daughter's laptop was intact.

Tapping the keys quickly, Linus located the data he was looking for, but the power requirements were beyond what he could use without being noticed. He pushed off from the table and spun around several times in his chair. So close. He was so close. He stopped. How had Trisia managed it without drawing attention from the local power company?

Linus leaned back in the chair and thought of the lab as he emerged from his prison. Something was out of place he realized, and he tried to remember what. It could have been Trisia had moved things around, but no she wouldn't have bothered. There was plenty of room. Plenty of room ... His mind's eye centered on a large squarish object sitting on one of the tables. It was not something he had put there, it must have been Trisia. In his mind he went over the object again and again. Then he remembered the object glowing when he arrived and even more intense when he triggered the warp to leave. *A power source? Hmm, if she built one ...*

Linus searched all the data he had uploaded from the old lab and came across plans for a device called a power cell. *Ah-ha!* But as he looked over the various schematics, he frowned. *There is no way she could have come up with this on her own. No matter, it will do what I need.*

Linus checked his equipment. He had most of the required components, although a few would have to acquire. He logged into a shell corporation he had set up long ago and ordered the parts, specifying the at the local delivery office as the destination. He ticked the next day rush and sat back. Soon he would have all he needed.

The air conditioner in Keleeigan's lab kicked on, sending a chill down Red's back. She pulled the zipper on her full-length bodysuit all the way up, sat on the sofa next to Trisia, and chewed the inside of her cheek. They had to go after Linus, any delay was unacceptable. And yet she knew if they ran headlong after him, there would likely be a nasty surprise waiting. These two sides of her fought like giant sumo wrestlers, each one trying to gain the upper hand.

She could take no more and stood up. "Atrus, where are the coordinates you detected earlier? I'm going to after Sanford."

Professor Keleeigan, Atrus and James looked at her. "I don't think that is wise," Keleeigan said.

"I concur. We need more data," Atrus said.

James sighed. "While I have no desire to be trapped again like a rat in a cage, I feel as Red, we need to go after him. If we wait too long, who knows where he will pop up again."

"If he uses the dimensional transporter again, we will know the instant a warp is opened, and the coordinates," Atrus said.

"Not to mention, it takes a vast amount of power to generate such warps. He only has access to common sources of power, if he tries to pull that much from the grid it will light up warning boards all over the east coast."

"Unless he finds away around it," Red said.

Trisia stood and shook her head. "I had the same problem, the only way I could find a way around it was to use the professors power cell."

"My power cell …" Keleeigan muttered before turning back to his keyboard. He punched in a few search commands and frowned. "Atrus, can you determine if the files in this folder under documents were copied from Trisia's backup?" Keleeigan pointed to a spot on the lower left of his screen.

Atrus nodded. "I can, one moment." He closed his eyes to open them three seconds later. "I had to access the main server where the backup is stored as the data shown to us was not enough to make such a–"

"Atrus! Were they accessed?"

"Yes, they were. From what I can tell, all data from those folders, along with the files inside the parent folder were transmitted."

"Shit," Keleeigan muttered under his breath.

James looked at him. "Doc? What does that mean?"

Trisia stepped forward to see where Keleeigan pointed and sighed. "That's where I stored all the plans and data for his power cell."

"Meaning, he has *my* device!" Keleeigan said through gritted teeth

"Maybe he won't realize he has it," James said.

Keleeigan's head snapped around. "He's not stupid. He may be insane, but he has demonstrated his raw intelligence has not been affected yet. I am sure he checked through all the data at the first opportunity."

"Time to go," Red said as she started up the stairs.

James held out his hand. "Now wait a sec, it will still take him time to build one, and get it working."

Trisia nodded. "Yes, it took me months to build mine."

"But you don't have a background in such technology. Linus does. And he worked with me, so he will figure out my methodology even sooner," Keleeigan said.

"James, grab Atrus, we are going," Red said.

James sighed, picked up Atrus' cylindrical unit from the table, slipped it into the holster under his arm, and grabbed his backpack from alongside the couch. "I know we don't want to wait too long but I still think going now is a mistake. We have a few days at least, and you haven't completely recovered from the last jump."

"I'm fine and waiting would be the mistake. We now know he has the means to generate more dimensional warps. Who knows what kind of damage he could do."

Trisia approached. "I'm coming too. You might need my help."

Red looked back. "I doubt it, and the more people I take, the longer I have to hold the warp open. The longer I hold the warp open, the more it drains me."

"Let her come." They all looked back at Keleeigan, who sat with his arms folded. "She knows Linus better than anyone, except me. She might be of assistance. I would go, but my knees aren't that good these days. I would only slow you down. And I will try to get my system operational while you are gone. It might be handy."

James nodded. "Right Doc, we will be back soon."

"You had better. I still have to download the plans from the gun in your holster."

James spun around. "I thought you did that long ago?"

Keleeigan gestured over the mess of equipment in his basement. "When have I had time?"

James chuckled as he continued up the stairs. "You have a point."

9

Linus sat back, viewing the world through blurry eyes. He had spent the entire night working on the power cell. While the rest of the components would arrive later today, this made sure the device would be operational as soon as possible.

He didn't expect to have the device ready except for the missing components so soon. But the basic design proved simpler than he first thought. Once he recognized his old colleague's methods, the rest fell into place. And having a large stockpile of equipment on hand helped.

Linus gazed over at the large analogue clock on the wall. It was still early morning, and the delivery wouldn't arrive until the afternoon. He stretched and decided it was time for lunch. The egg rolls and fortune cookies had long since disappeared. He grabbed some cash from a drawer and headed for the elevator.

A lightning bolt landed in the center between two buildings, leaving a glowing crack in its wake. The crack quickly expanded into a rip in space and time large enough for a person to pass through. James crashed out and rolled to the side a second before Trisia fell out on to the spot where he was. "Roll to the other side!" James said.

"What? Why–" She didn't have time to answer before Red crashed out of the warp and landed on top of her. The warp grew for a second, then slammed shut with a loud *boom*.

"I tried to tell you."

Red rolled off and stood up. "If Atrus is right, this is where Sanford arrived."

"I am correct. I would not have told you if the probability of error was high."

James looked around. "Atrus? What? No hologram?"

"I detect several people approaching our location. I suggest everyone *look natural*, I believe is the phrase."

James offered his hand and pulled Trisia to her feet. "Like he said, act natural."

Two police officers walked into the alleyway. Their badges caught the light reflecting it in several directions on their otherwise dark, almost black uniforms with matching hats. The patches and badges showed they were from the Anchorage PD. "Hello folks. Is everything all right?"

"Yes. Why would you ask?" James said.

"We heard a loud bang and I thought I saw an electrical arc a few seconds ago. We thought there might have been an explosion." His eyes drifted up and down the walls of the two buildings, but didn't see any sign of damage.

"We didn't see anything like that."

The other officer eyed him. "I would like to hear from the ladies if you don't mind."

Red shook her head. "Nope, I didn't see anything like that. Did you Trisia?"

"Nope. I didn't either."

"Uh-huh," the second officer said, then looked at his

partner. "If it is all the same to you, would you all mind coming with us? We have a few more questions."

James straightened and reached into his jacket. Both officers drew their guns and pointed them at him. "Not so fast. Remove the hand right now. Nice and slow," the first trooper said.

James' fingers pulled out a wallet and flipped it open. The large FBI logo and his photo visible even with the distance between them. "I'm agent Moknkin on special assignment. These two ladies are assisting me. Would you mind lowering your weapons?"

Both officers nodded and holstered their weapons. "Sorry sir, we had to be sure. There was a report of something odd here last night."

Red stepped forward. "Something odd? Could you be more specific?"

The first trooper nodded. "Well, yes and no. All we know is we had a report of a loud noise and what looked like electrical discharges from here. But we found nothing."

James looked at Red and Trisia. They all nodded. He turned back towards the troopers. "While I appreciate your department's assistance, I am now taking over this investigation. What you have seen is classified and you are not to discuss it with anyone else. Is that understood?"

"We understand. But this is the first time I've seen an FBI agent in Alaska. Are you sure you are on the right track?"

James gave a glare, telling the officer all he needed to know. "Right." He looked to his partner and made a motion with his head. "Come on, we have a beat to finish." They both left a second later.

"Well that was close," Trisia said.

James looked around the corner to make sure they had left,

then turned back. "We have had worse. But you heard them. It is certain Sanford was here."

"As I told you," Atrus said.

"Didn't doubt you. But you weren't 100% certain," Red said.

"100% certainty is very difficult given the number of unknown variables," Atrus replied.

"So what do we do now?" Trisia said, peeking around the corner.

"Don't look at us, you are the supposed Sanford expert," Red said.

"Well it is obvious, he didn't enter the coordinates that landed inside his lab."

"Obviously," Red grunted.

"He must have it somewhere nearby. I know he wouldn't want it to be too far away, in case he was seen and had to make a run for it."

Red nodded. "Makes sense. Now where would such a lab be? Assuming it is why he came here."

Trisia looked back. "I suspected he had another one. You see, he gave me a lot of money to make sure I had the funds to build what I needed to rescue him. But I always had the feeling he was holding back. And if it was his only lab, he wouldn't have blown it up. He would have done everything he could to save it."

"She has a point," James said. "There is no doubt he plans ahead. Even several steps ahead, and for various contingencies."

Trisia nodded. "Yes. And I am sure, wherever this lab is, it is not in a location that would see much traffic. He would want to slip in and out without being noticed. I'm sure he suspects you will go after him. Or if you didn't survive, someone else will. And being you did track and find me, there is little doubt it is possible. So he will keep a low profile."

"Anything else? Perhaps something we don't know, like his habits?"

"He might have worked through the night, but if he did he will eat something before going back."

James smiled. "Which means a restaurant."

Trisia nodded. "Yes."

They exited the space between the buildings and James pointed to the fast-food restaurant across the street. "Looks like as a good a place as any." They crossed the street, opened the door, and entered.

Linus walked, shoulders slumped into town. He kept his head down. The fewer people saw him, the better. His stomach growled and he looked for a restaurant. After looking at several, he headed towards the same one he used last night as they had already seen him. Or at least the night shift had.

People passed him but didn't look too close. His short-sleeve shirt, baggy pants and an old thin jacket he had found in the lab didn't make him look like a local out for a walk. Something he would have to fix. He reached the Chinese restaurant and pulled the doors open.

10

James looked at the line of people and sighed. "I could use my badge, but it will draw attention from everyone here. And sooner or later it will get back to Sanford.

Trisia smiled. "Leave it to me." She walked past the people in line and inserted herself at the counter. The girl behind the counter rolled her eyes and was about to speak when Trisia made eye contact with a man near the drink dispensers. He was about twenty by the look of him, tired and bored out of his skull. His eyes drifted up from her tight jeans to a tight yellow scoop necked shirt and light black jacket. She flashed a winning smile and blinked several times. "Excuse me, could you help me for a second?"

The man walked over. "I'm sorry Miss, you will have to wait in line like everyone else." He pointed to the line of people already starting to get irritated at her presence.

Trisia blinked her long eyelashes again. "What? Oh, no, I'm not here to eat. I am looking for my Father." She pulled out a small red bifold wallet from the pocket of her jeans, flipped it open to a picture, and held it out.

The man leaned forward, looking at the image of Trisia with an older man smiling at the camera and holding his arm around her. "No, I am sorry. I haven't seen him."

Trisia pulled the picture from her wallet and held it out again. "Are you sure? He might have come through sometime last night. Please take a good look."

"I'm sure and I have been here all night. He didn't come in here." The man looked both ways and leaned closer. "I get off in an hour. Will you be around?"

Trisia flashed her winning smile. "Maybe, if I can find him. Are there many other places open late around here?"

"Sure, most of us do these days. Have to. Once one started it, the rest all had to follow or look like they're out-of-date."

"I see. Thanks for your help." Trisia turned back towards Red and James.

"Wait, will I see you later?"

Trisia looked back over her shoulder. "Maybe." She winked and continued walking.

"You enjoyed that a little too much," Red said with a lopsided grin.

"Maybe, maybe not. But I did find out he wasn't here."

They walked outside and looked up and down the street as cars drove past. "Where to next?" Red asked.

"I know he must have stopped somewhere to eat. No way he could have gone this long without eating something."

"If I may suggest, at this moment there is an individual entering the Chinese restaurant several buildings down who matches my records of Linus Sanford," Atrus whispered.

"Atrus! How do you know it is him?"

"I have accessed the security systems of all the buildings in the area, and he has entered said location a moment ago."

"Why didn't you mention this as an option we started looking?" Red said.

"You didn't ask."

"Atrus! What did I say about not telling us important information like this?"

"I told you as soon as I could confirm. As for why I didn't previously, my capabilities would take an hour or more to list."

"But you could have offered before we started looking. That is what I am talking about."

"As I said, I did. The timing of offering such information is a work in progress."

"Atrus, you and I are going to have a long talk later," James growled.

"If I may suggest, he is about to exit the building. It may be wise to not be so visible when he does?" Atrus said.

"Right," Red said as they moved behind the vacant teller booth of the movie theater next door. A moment later they saw Sanford in the same clothes, save a light jacket with the collar pulled up around his neck and a hat pulled down low. "And you are sure it is him?"

"Identity is verified. It is Linus Sanford. If you like, I could run a full scan."

Red raised her hand. "No, if you do that, the green beam will let him know we are watching."

"I know. But you said you wanted options. See? I am offering them."

Red rolled her eyes and nudged James. "Yes, you two need a serious talk."

"Don't I know it," James said never taking his eyes off of Sanford. The man looked up and down the street then took off heading in the other direction carrying two oyster pails of takeout.

"Glad he didn't come this way," Trisia said pointing, "and

he is not eating there, he must be heading back to his new lab. All we have to do is follow."

"Yes. But easier said then done," James said. "He is certain to be checking for anyone following. At the moment, it isn't too difficult to keep out of sight. But I know the buildings get far less dense the further you go on this road." Red looked at James. "What? I did some of my training up here. And be thankful this is not in the dead of winter. Last time I froze parts of me I didn't know existed."

Trisia blinked. "Oh?"

James turned towards the shorter woman on his right. "Never mind."

Sanford continued to move with the intent of a man on his first mission. He paused every two buildings to feign interest at something inside for a few seconds, then look up and down the street. So far they had managed to keep from being seen, but were running out of buildings.

Red looked at the lack of cover and glared at James. "Now what, Mr. FBI?"

James' eyes narrowed. He hated being called that. And she hadn't in so long. He was about to give a retort when he saw the gleam in her teasing eye. "How about we let someone else trail him?"

Trisia blinked. "Who?"

James unslung his backpack, reached inside, and pulled out a cone-shaped device with a protruding half-spherical section almost the size of a volleyball instead of the usual flat area at the other end. He pressed a hidden button, a panel slid open, he powered on the device, and pushed the button again sealing the opening. The Shell levitated off his hand.

"Oh, that thing. I forgot about it," Trisia said.

James smiled. "Yes. Atrus, do you have control of the Shell?"

"If I didn't, it would not be levitating off of your hand," Atrus said.

Trisia blinked. "Shell?"

"Spherical Hovering Energized Laser Level is the original term. However, this unit has been–"

James grimaced. "Atrus! Activate the cloak and follow Sanford."

"Acknowledged." The Shell flickered for a second, then disappeared. "Shell has acquired Sanford and is following. I can give you a visual if you wish."

James looked around. "Not here. For now, keep us apprised of his movements. We need to know where he is going."

"Understood."

"We can't stay here, we look too conspicuous." James pointed to the lingerie shop across the road. "We can go in there."

Red glared. "Are you nuts? We might fit in, but a guy in a black suit in a lingerie store is going to draw more attention than we want."

"Nah, I am just buying my girlfriend something nice for her birthday."

Red's eyes narrowed. "Something for *you*, you mean."

Trisia raised a finger. "Umm so which one of us is your girlfriend?" They both turned and glared at her. "Geez sorry I asked. I just wanted to have our story straight."

"Fine. This time I came prepared." He reached into his backpack again, this time pulling out a tiny device no larger than a quarter of an inch. He popped the device in his ear, handed one to both women and smiled. "Atrus, do you have access to the A.T.E.?"

Trisia looked down at the tiny flesh-colored device in her hand. "What's an A.T.E.?"

"It is short for Autonomous Translating Earpiece. While only designed as a translator, I have enhanced the device in several ways. One being improved tracking for the body's movements during holographic usage. I assume you would like me to project a disguise on you?" Atrus said.

"Yes. A female one if you please," James said.

Trisia blinked and James' body reformed into a tall blonde woman wearing dark black pants and a tight white sweater. "Wow. You can be a girl too? That's amazing."

"Yes, isn't it?" James said.

"Hold on. You won't fool anyone with that voice. Not to mention your walk and motions will give you away three seconds after we get in there." Red rolled her eyes. "This is too weird."

James shrugged. "Okay, have it your way." The image fell away, and he gestured towards the store. "Ladies, after you."

Red said nothing but a grunt as she popped the A.T.E. into her ear and started walking across the street. James and Trisia followed, but half-way across she leaned closer. "What, are you two having issues or something?"

James leaned over. "I had to find clothes for her once, and I got the wrong size."

"Ohhhh, that explains it."

"Yeah, it wasn't pretty, and she won't let me forget it either."

"Perhaps she will forgive you yet."

"Oh she has, she just can't help holding it over my head."

Red stood in front of the store's glass window. The mannequins within displayed several styles of lingerie, from lacy teddies to satin bra and panty sets. She turned, leaned back against the window, and folded her arms. "What are you two talking about?"

Trisia smiled. "Nothing much. Just the breeze that whipped through. I could swear I smelled Italian."

"Actually, they were–"

James gritted his teeth. "Atrus!"

"–discussing how to proceed inside."

"Uh-huh." Red said as she pushed herself off of the window.

James grabbed the door, held it open for both women, and followed them inside. One of the ladies behind the counter smiled and ran over to them. "Welcome, can I help you?"

"Yes, I need to pick up something for my girlfriend," James said.

The woman cocked her head to one side then the other as she looked at Red, then Trisia. "And which one might that be?" With the receipt of several glares the sales woman backed up. "Right. Take your time. If you need anything, I will be right here." She pointed to a display three feet away, walked over, and proceeded to unpack a recent shipment.

Red and Trisia stood there for several minutes and the two clerks gave them several looks. James leaned closer. "I think you two had better look like you are trying to find something."

"The Shell has traced Sanford to his new base of operations. I suggest finding something to try on and use one of the changing rooms. I can display my findings there," Atrus whispered.

"Sounds like a good idea to me."

"You would!" Red grabbed a lacy red teddy off of the nearest rack and walked over to the woman behind the counter. "Where are your fitting rooms please?"

She pointed to a hidden recessed area in the one corner. "Over there."

"Thank you." Red headed for them, with Trisia and James following along. Both of the clerks gave suspicious glances but then shrugged. It was more common these days than it used to be.

Inside the compact room, Trisia and James pressed themselves against the walls. Red shut the door, flipped the lock, and tossed the teddy on a small shelf mounted next to the full-length mirror. "Atrus, show us what you found."

In the middle of the room Atrus projected a small image of Sanford approaching a building in a very obvious condemned state. In the back, Sanford entered a working elevator and disappeared.

"No way that is working with the rest of the building looking like a junk pile unless his lab is in there," James said.

"Confirmed. It is in the basement. If you notice the indicator of the elevator is going down. And being this is the ground floor, that leaves a basement."

Red rolled her eyes. "Forgive him, he has been reading Sherlock Holmes."

"But he is right," James said.

Her eyes narrowed. "He doesn't need your help."

"So what's our next move?" Trisia asked.

"Simple, we go and get him," Red said.

"Now wait a second. Remember his last lab? He must have security in there. We will need to be very careful or it might blow up in our faces."

"I doubt it. This is his second lab. Do you think he has more? Backups are one thing, but a tertiary backup on that scale?" Red shook her head. "No way."

"I have to agree," James said. "I can't see how he would have any more locations."

Trisia shrugged. "If you say so. I think he would, but I guess it's just me."

"Are you okay in there? Do you need any help?" A muffled voice called.

"Yes, we're fine. We'll be out in a minute," Red said in an elevated voice. "I think we have overstayed our welcome," she grabbed the teddy off the shelf, "time to go."

They nodded and exited the changing room one by one. Red smiled at the clerk watching the door and handed her the teddy. "Not what I was looking for. Thanks anyway." The woman gave a strange look as they all left the store.

They made their way outside of town and carefully approached the derelict building with its one working elevator. It had once been a large factory of some sort, but now sat empty. Architectural bones left with nothing to protect. Several areas of the ceiling had fallen in, but the area near the back showed less rubble or dirt.

They stepped through an enormous hole in a side wall, trying to not trip over the bricks that once filled it. The elevator sat unlit and motionless in the middle of the back wall. The place still looked empty. But looks can be deceiving. "Atrus? I assume he has a security system in place?" James said.

"Yes. One hidden camera is pointed at the elevator and I have detected motion detectors in the area, but it should be a simple procedure to disable them."

Red's eyes narrowed. "Without destroying them?"

"That would be more difficult."

"She's right. If they go offline, I suspect it will trigger an alarm," James said.

"I could attempt to lure him out by intentionally tripping said devices," Atrus said.

"And let him know we are here? No, there has to be another way."

"One moment. It appears he is exiting the lab." Red, James, and Trisia moved back through the hole to watch from the corner of a dirty, broken window. The elevator doors opened and Linus Sanford stepped out. He looked around and took off heading for town.

"Wonder what he is such a hurry for?" Red said.

"Whatever it is, it can't be good. But now is our chance. Atrus, can you get us inside?"

"Affirmative."

"Good. While you look inside, I will see what he is in such a hurry for," Red said.

"But he will see you," Trisia said.

Red smiled. "No, he won't. You forget I can move fast." They blinked and Red was gone in a blast of wind.

Trisia's mouth fell open, but she quickly closed it. "I didn't know she could do *that*."

"Yeah, she doesn't like to as it drains her energy. But it has come in handy on more than one occasion. Atrus? Which is the best way to approach the elevator?"

Atrus' flashed on in front of them. "It doesn't matter. The devices will not detect you."

James' eyes narrowed. "But I thought we told you not to?"

"I didn't disable the devices, which might have set off an alarm."

"Then what did you do?"

"I used the Shell's holographic matrix to cover them. They will not detect anything at the moment," his image flickered and vanished.

James smiled. "Nice move." He looked at Trisia and tilted his head in the direction of the elevator. "Come on." They ran to the doors and stood in front of them. "I assume I can't just push a button?"

"Correct. However, I do have a solution." The Shell's cloak deactivated and the device hovered in the air. It moved to the right of the access panel and it opened to reveal a keypad, and a little two-inch screen extended above it. The Shell moved closer and the nose touched the metal of the keypad. A moment later "Access Granted" in green letters on the little screen and the doors slid open.

They slipped inside, the Shell joined them, and the elevator began to descend. Ten seconds later the doors opened again to a large open space with tables, computational cores, and several screens displayed various programs executing pre-set tasks. Everything the previous lab had and more. James began to take a step, but Atrus flashed on in front of him. "I wouldn't do that."

"What?"

"Leave the elevator. I have detected several more security devices, and cameras in the area."

Trisia's eyes went wide. "Then he already knows we are here."

"Negative, I enabled a holographic image at the front of the elevator. As far as the devices are concerned, the elevator doors never opened."

"Now what? We can't stay in here forever."

Atrus smiled. "Correct, but I only need a few more minutes to disable these devices as well." The Shell's cloak enabled and it slid out into the room. It hovered around, stopping at various locations. Once to every corner of the room, then into areas beneath several tables. "It is now safe to enter. These devices are simpler and easy to lock into a continuous loop of data."

"Thanks Atrus," James said as Atrus' image disappeared.

They walked among all the different tables of equipment. Along one wall held several squarish devices. Wires hung out from the corners and they looked unfinished. "What are these? It looks like he is making several of them, whatever they are."

Trisia walked over and peered inside the plastic boxes. "Power cells! All of them are the Professor's power cells. But a few bits are missing."

Atrus appeared. "I concur, these devices are very similar to Professor Keleeigan's design."

"Why would he need a bunch of them? It doesn't make sense."

Red's voice came loud and clear into James' ear. "James? Do you hear me?"

"Yes, I do. A.T.E.s are working fine."

"If you are inside the lab, get out now! He will be back in a couple of minutes unless you want me to stop him. But then he will know we are here."

"No, don't. I think we can hide down here."

"What for? Just have the Shell blast everything important in the room. It should still have enough power."

Atrus nodded. "It does."

"Then do it."

"Red, look, he is up to something. Something big. We found ten nearly completed power cells."

"Ten? What the heck? He would only need one."

"Right, and we can't find out if we leave. If we destroy the place, he builds another one somewhere else we don't know about, and figures out how to stop us from tracking him. Then what?"

"That would not be possible," Atrus said.

"Atrus! We don't know, it might be. We do know his warps are very different."

"You have a point. He is almost to the elevator. Hide."

Trisia looked around and pointed to the storage area. "I bet we can hide in there."

"Good idea. Atrus? Should we be cloaked as well?"

"Negative. There is not an obvious way to view the area unless you are inside it. I do not wish to drain the Shell's resources any more than needed."

James nodded as they ran for the U shaped area along the far wall, slipped within the narrow entrance, and squatted down.

A few minutes later the elevator doors ground open to reveal Sanford carrying several boxes. He walked over to one of the empty tables and set down the boxes. He grabbed a box cutter and slit the packing tape. Flipping the flaps up, he withdrew ten circuit boards sealed in electrostatic safe bags. Smiling, he slit open the bags, examining the boards under a magnifier mounted on a spring-loaded arm.

Seeing everything was as he expected, he walked over to the table with the power cells and began to plug the boards into them. After a few minutes, the device's glowed bright blue.

Trisia pointed and mouthed, "They're operational."

James nodded. The Shell could take him out with one shot, but he couldn't be certain it would stop whatever he was planning.

"James? Can you hear me? Is everything okay?" came

through the earpiece. He wanted to tell her to be quiet, but he couldn't say anything without being heard.

"We are fine. He cannot respond without giving away our position," Atrus said into Red's earpiece.

Sanford appeared to pause for a second, then continued. In another minute every one of the power cells was online and their housings sealed. He walked over to the nearest keyboard and tapped in a few commands. A second later a red grid of intense energy enveloped the storage area.

"I know you are there. You might as well say hello," Sanford said.

"How?" Trisia said standing up.

"Ah, Trisia, my darling. You survived. I thought it might be possible after you had told me of these people." He walked over to the entrance of the storage area. "Hmm only two of you? Where is the other one?"

James stood up. "Gone. She went for help."

Sanford laughed. "Do you expect me to believe that? Who could she get? The local police? Keleeigan? Doesn't matter anyway, by the time they arrive, I will be long gone." He turned away and approached a table on his left.

"Gone where?" Trisia asked.

Sanford turned back around. "Wouldn't you like to know?"

"I would."

"Well, guess." Sanford smiled again, spun back around, and started stuffing the power cells into a large bag.

"If you won't tell us what you are up to, then how about how you knew we were here?" James said.

Sanford looked over his shoulder. "I suppose I could give you that. I always make it a habit to view my security systems when I return. I noticed a fly kept landing in the exact same spot over and over again. Now either he was going crazy, the cheap Russian junk broke, or someone tampered with it. I assumed the latter." He looked towards the far wall and smiled. "Time for me to go. I will bid you both adieu."

"Aw come on. A guy like you isn't going to gloat?"

"Nope. I don't need to. I have you beat."

"You only think you do. Atrus, take out this grid please."

The Shell decloaked and several high-intensity red beams shot out from now-extended points on its otherwise smooth underside. Each beam hit with increased power at a corresponding location where the cage holding them in, intersected. After the sixth shot, the energy grid overloaded and fell away, but by this time Sanford slung the bag over his shoulder and activated a different almost flat square device now on his chest. He pushed another button and a flash of energy erupted from the device, hitting the wall in front of him and expanding into a green and black swirling vortex.

"Atrus! Stop him!" James said, pulling the gun from the holster under his arm.

"The Shell's energy is depleted, I cannot fire again until it recharges."

"Shit!" James yelled as he flipped open the control panel in the grip to reduce the power level to stun.

"I won't let you get between me and my revenge," Sanford said before jumping into the circular mass of energy and disappeared.

"Atrus? What did we just see?"

"It would appear Linus Sanford has not only perfected his dimensional door, but also made it portable."

The elevator opened, and Red stepped out. "What happened?"

James sighed. "I am trying to find that out. Atrus?"

"I did not have time to scan the device on his chest. But

I would assume it is a portable and more powerful version of what Trisia used to pull him from the dimension he was trapped in."

"But how would he power it?" Trisia asked.

"He must have used one of the power cells, but a smaller one we didn't see him activate. I also regret to inform you it would appear he has made several alterations making tracking his signature through the dimensional door difficult." Atrus said.

"Great, not only did you fail to stop him, he could be anywhere in the world and jump again any time he wants," Red said.

"Negative, I am certain such a dimensional jump must drain the power cell. It would need to recharge before another portal is possible."

"Still, he could be anywhere. Wait, he mentioned revenge. Atrus, get Doc," James said.

"James? What is going on?" Professor Keleeigan's voice hung in the air.

"Everything okay with you? Anything out of the ordinary? Or at your main lab?"

"Nope. Why? What happened?"

"We will tell you when we get back." A click was heard as the connection cut. "If he didn't go after Doc, where did he go?"

"Wait a sec. He told me he never intended on killing the President, but he had to make it look that way to satisfy his partners long enough to get us both away to safety," Trisia said.

James looked at her. "His partners? Who are they?"

Trisia shrugged. "I'm not sure, but a bunch of Russians came to testify he was dead at the hearing."

Red cocked her head. "Russians? Do you know where they are?"

"No, but I bet Keleeigan might have an idea."

11

Lightning struck, opening a crack which quickly expanded. James fell out onto the soft grass, rolling to the side, Trisia exited a second later, rolled the other way, Red landed with a thud. The warp shrank and disappeared.

Keleeigan walked off of his porch and towards them. "I take it didn't go very well? Atrus told me you were coming."

Red stood up. "You could say that."

"What happened?"

James stood up and grunted. "Well let's see, Sanford has your energy cell design, created a bunch of them, then slipped through our fingers."

"What!"

"Yes, and it gets worse. He has some sort of portable system to create the dimensional warps. That is how he escaped."

"Do you know where?"

Red shook her head. "No. We hoped you might have an idea."

"Me? I haven't worked with the man in over a decade. I thought Trisia was going along as the expert."

"I told them I'm not an expert. But I will help anyway I can," Trisia said. "All we know is he mentioned revenge. I thought it might be against his former colleagues. Do you have any idea who they might be?"

Keleeigan stroked his chin. "Not really. I had heard something which might suggest Russia, but that was more rumor."

"By the way, what could he do with ten of your power cells?" James said.

Keleeigan blinked. "Ten? Are you joking?"

James shook his head. "Wish I was. He had a bunch of them and I counted ten when he was installing components."

"I think there must have been one more. And don't forget the device he had on his chest. It must have had one," Trisia said.

"True. Doc, any idea what he could do with them?"

"There are a lot of things you could do with one. Let alone ten, I can't imagine. Heck I power an entire lab with ease with one."

"Are they dangerous?" Red asked.

"Not at all. I put a lot of protections."

"Could they be removed?"

"No." Keleeigan turned away, then back. His eyes narrowed. "I suppose in theory, if he shunted the precise frequency into the recovery system, an overload might be possible."

"And what would happen then?"

"The entire unit would explode."

"How big of an explosion?"

"Hmm, hard to say. But a rough guess, one would be one of them could take out thirty square miles."

James' eyes went wide. "Holy! Doc! What did you create?"

"Hey, the chances of that are almost nil. You would have

to rework much of the systems before the possibility would even exist."

"Want to bet Sanford did?"

"Maybe, but I doubt it."

"Say he did. Where would he be going if Russia was his target?"

"I don't know, it was just a rumor."

"I have a hunch it is more than a rumor. The colleagues that helped me declare him dead were Russian," Trisia said.

"Do you know who they were?"

Trisia shook her head. "No. They were secretive. At the time I thought they had traveled without letting their bosses know, now I wonder the true reason."

Keleeigan stroked his chin again. "Well, given the kind of money he would have needed to continue his work and develop the cloak, they must have very deep pockets."

"No kidding," Trisia said, "he gave me over five hundred million so I could get what I needed."

Keleeigan stared at her. "Five hundred million? I had a hunch he was working with another country, but this proves it. Only a very large country would have pockets that deep. Russia fits, and the only place in Russia I know of with access to that kind of money has to be the Federal Security Service. And I'm sure they would love a working cloaking system. Heck, any country would."

James bounced a hand off his forehead. "I'm an idiot! No doubt the FSB would do anything for a functional cloaking technology. And if they had any question of Sanford's commitment, would go out of their way to ensure his loyalty. Wait! If he is going after them, he must have gone to–"

Keleeigan nodded. "Right. Lubyanskya Square in the heart of Moscow."

"But if that many of your power cells overloaded there … "

"It would take out most of the city, if he spread them out."

James took a step back. "I wish we could confirm it is where he went."

Atrus' image flashed in front of them. "I can confirm he went to Lubyanskaya Square."

"What? How?"

"I am now able to track his dimensional crossings, given enough time, and I am near the location of the origin point at the moment of use."

"Well, why didn't you say so!"

"I believe I just did."

"No! I mean why didn't you mention it when we were trying to figure out where he is?"

"It took longer than before to ascertain his location. I detected some interference this time, and it caused disruptions making the final destination difficult," Atrus said as his image disappeared.

"Looks like we are going to Russia," James said. He looked at Red. "Are you up to it?"

"Of course. Local warps are not a problem. Temporal warps are what drain me." Red walked to the middle of Keleeigan's back yard and lowered herself to a sprinting position. "Get ready." She took off running faster and faster. The air began to swirl and Keleeigan moved back to his deck.

Clouds rolled in, and Red increased her speed again. Lightning struck the center, and a rip opened in the fabric of space and time. The rip blossomed into a full warp two seconds later. "Go!" Red shouted.

Trisia and James ran for the warp and jumped in with Red following a second later.

Behind a building the air swirled as a green rip between dimensions spread out and Linus Sanford stepped through. The energy horizon flickered, flashed, and collapsed in upon itself when he was three steps away.

Linus' head swiveled around as his eyes adapted to the dark star-lit sky. He squinted at a location further down the street and smiled. His target lay some distance away, lit by the various street lights and decorative lighting dotting the windows. His smile widened as he began walking towards it. Being this late at night, it will be easy.

The air had the same feel as the last time he was here, a time that did not go very well, but now he had the advantage. He flipped the collar up on his jacket and smiled. He continued on for several steps, pressed a button on the device on his belt, and disappeared.

The air rippled as a lightning bolt shot down, leaving a crack in its wake. The crack expanded, contracted then expanded again, leaving a swirling mass of temporal energy. Trisia fell out and rolled out of the way a second before James and Red followed. The warp slammed shut behind them.

James looked around but didn't see anyone. "Good, no one saw us land."

"I can imagine trying to explain that one. How do you do it?" Trisia said.

"We don't. Or at least we haven't yet."

Red smiled. "I can guide us while inside the warp, I try to target areas without many people. But I will admit it is difficult at times."

In the distance, bells could be heard coming from St. Sophia's. James sighed as he tried to get his bearings. "I'm not as familiar with Russia as I should be. Atrus, are we in the correct location?"

"Yes Sir, although temporally we seem off by a day. I checked the local time when we landed."

Red nodded. "I figured this time we had better get here before he does."

"But that means there are two of us here now."

"Yes, so make sure you don't call yourself or Keleeigan or we will intrude on our own time-lines."

Trisia blinked. "I assume it would be bad?"

"Yes, very. I did it once, and trust me when I say you do not want to. If it is bad enough, it could destroy you and the space-time continuum. Although we might get lucky and it would only affect this galaxy."

"Atrus? I assume you speak Russian?"

"Indeed. And through the earpieces, so will you."

"Good, because we are about to put it to the test."

A man in non-distinct clothing walked over to them. "Hello, is there a problem?"

"No, not at all why?"

"I saw you standing here for some time and not moving. Most tourists have cameras are always moving and taking pictures. You are not doing either."

"Oh, well we like to take our time. Is that okay?"

The man smiled. "By all means. Enjoy." He walked away towards the south and out of sight.

"He has not disappeared and is still watching. I suggest we move and try to be enamored of the area," Atrus whispered.

"Of course," James said, "I suppose we do not exactly fit

in with Red's skin-tight bodysuit, my suit and Trisia in tight jeans and a t-shirt."

"I would give you new appearance, but we would be seen."

"Save your energy Atrus, we might need it later. What's the status of the Shell?"

"I am not certain at the moment as it is in full power-down mode, but given the time it has been in said mode it should now have a quarter of capacity," Atrus said.

Director Kirov sat in his office on the top floor of the FSB. "More paperwork." He grumbled reading and checking across several paper forms on his desk. He looked over at the computer to his right. "You would think we would be doing away with this." While Russia had made many strides, like everywhere else, paper in government seemed to be a fact of life. No matter how hard they tried to remove paper, it continued. Often increasing, rather than less. Kirov's eyes drifted up to the clock on the wall. It was late. While a few bright stars still twinkled through the fog of city lights, the sky reflected a tapestry of perfect night otherwise. His neck cracked and his muscles complained, but this had to be done first.

The report contained several strange occurrences with the Americans. The odd part, it was not something easily detectable. Over the last year, those that worked with Sanford had tried to duplicate his technology without success. They remained baffled by it. Apparently, he left just enough information out of his logs to prevent someone duplicating the work without him.

Kirov gritted his teeth. Sanford was a loose cannon from

the start. But if successful, what they paid for would give dividends for many years to come. No one had any of the devices he had proposed. And the cloaking system was the first, and best of many. *And* it worked! Only to lose him and the prototype. No one wanted to tell him when it happened, and he wanted to tell those above him even less. At least he still had his position, but if another prototype could not be made, he might find himself in a hidden location of Siberia. Or worse.

"Yes, you would think paper would be an endangered species by now," a voice called.

Kirov looked around, but no one was in the room. "Who's there?" His head swiveled in several directions. His intercom was off, his door was closed, and he knew this room was soundproofed. He looked around the room again.

Nothing.

"The stress must be getting to me," Kirov muttered.

"Nope, you have your mind. But not for long."

Kirov stood up. "Who said that!"

"Why Ivan, I am shocked and hurt you don't recognize my voice."

Kirov's brow furrowed. "Sanford?"

"Congrats! You got it on the first try. Of course, I had to help you along."

Kirov's hands balled into fists. "I don't know who is playing this joke, but when I find them, they are going to wish they had never been born."

"I assure you Mr. Director, this is no joke. And I will prove it to you. Keep your eyes forward or you might miss it."

"What–" Before Kirov could finish, the air in front of him changed. At first there was a slight shimmer coming from the other side of his desk, then it rippled further as the dark outline of a man formed between the ripples. As each wave washed over him, he appeared more solid and details began to form. "Sanford! You are alive!"

"I am. No thanks to you."

"But I–"

"You forced me to use the cloak before I was ready. Not to mention you planned to have me, how shall we say it, 'removed' from the project after my 'demonstration' finished. Even if I did what you said."

"Ha! If you think I am going to fall for this, you are very mistaken. I know you never planned on executing the American President. We discovered it early on and took precautions."

"I know."

Kirov blinked, then a grin slid across his face. "Then you have come to kill me. I think you will find that hard to do when you are dead."

Sanford threw his head back and laughed. "Oh Kirov, I do miss your sense of humor," he raised a weapon and pointed it, "but not much."

Kirov's smile didn't wane. "Do you think you can shoot me? By now my security has seen this image and will be in here before your next breath."

"They might have, if I didn't disable the camera in your room. It was rather simple procedure, you really should have it fixed. I mean, anyone can walk in here and kill you."

This time Kirov's smile started to fade. "The sound will bring them then. You will only get off one shot. You had better make it a good one."

"Ah my dear Director, I am surprised you don't recognize this little device. I mean, you gave it to me after all. Or rather, one of your minions did."

Kirov's eyes went wide at the realization. The ricin pistol! "You will kill me, but you will not get out of here alive. I only have to press a button and the entire FSB will rain down upon you like a hurricane."

"Oh, I doubt that." Sanford fired and a pellet imbedded itself into Kirov's neck.

"You are a dead man." Kirov turned and reached for the button under his desk, but stopped. A strange tingle started in his neck then raced out to encompass his entire body in less than a second. He couldn't move. He couldn't even blink.

"By now you are wondering what happened my dear Director? Well, let me tell you, I didn't use ricin. As you know, I hate ricin. It is such an ugly death. I wouldn't wish that even on you. I did create an alternate pellet able to deliver a similar reaction in a little while, but non-fatal. However, for you I created this one. Do you like it? It is a neural paralyzer, but keeps you awake for the big finale! This, my dear Director, is payback for having your minions change the labeling on my pellets. I almost killed someone without knowing. By the way, how did you manage it? Oh right, you can't answer. Oh well trust me when I say, the question will not weigh heavily on my heart. But I will tell you the paralyzer has no long-term effects. If I had turned up the dosage, it would have stopped your heart. But where's the fun in that?"

Sanford walked over to a nearby chair and slid into it. "Oh, you don't mind if I sit down, do you?" Kirov stood there like a statue. "I didn't think so. By now I bet you are wondering what my big finish is? I would tell you, but I think will leave it as a surprise instead. I know how much you like surprises." He stood up, walked over to Kirov, and he leaned close. "But I will tell you this, the way you die will stay as one of the top news stories for the next several centuries. But enough hints." He padded the stiff man's shoulder. "I bid you adieu. Enjoy your front-row seat."

Sanford walked over to the door and started to turn the knob when he looked back. "Oh, if you were hoping someone would notice your lack of communication and come visit. I took the precaution of altering your schedule, saying you are not to be disturbed. Granted, they still might but I doubt it."

Sanford pulled open the door, stepped through, and stopped. His chin turned to touch his shoulder as his eyes jetted to the frozen figure behind him.

"And one more thing, I lied about disabling your cameras. I disabled all of your men. Or at least most of them a few seconds after they checked in. They won't be conscious for at least another twenty minutes, and by that time I will be long gone. But then so will you. Enjoy your once-in-a-lifetime experience, Director."

As the door closed Kirov's one eye quivered, and a tear slipped out.

James noticed the guard wasn't moving. Everything was fine the last time he had walked past the front of the FSB building, but now the man didn't move. Didn't even blink. He looked around and walked inside. The holographic bubble around him projected what would behind. He was, for all intents and purposes, cloaked. He took the man's wrist, a heart did beat, his breathing continued, but far slower than normal. James raised a finger and tapped the tiny nub inside his right ear. "Red? I think Sanford is here."

"What? How could he be? We have been watching long before he could have got here."

"I know, but I found a man just standing here like a statue."

"Where?"

"In the front lobby."

"You went *inside?*"

"Well, I couldn't check his pulse otherwise. He's alive, but appears frozen in place."

Trisia tapped the nub inside her ear. "I know he didn't get past me here." She had taken up a position on the other corner of the building. "I can see two sides of it and there isn't much traffic. No way he could have slipped past. Wait, you said inside?"

"Yes."

"How did he get inside without setting off every alarm?"

"An excellent question. Atrus? Access the building's security system. We need to know what is going on."

"I offered the suggestion before, and you declined. I told you I would not be detected," Atrus said.

"Yeah, yeah, we know. Just do it," Red said.

"I have accessed the system. It would appear all the people I can locate in this building are not moving."

"Atrus, what happened to them?"

"Please hold me out so I may perform an intensive scan."

James removed Atrus' cylinder from the pocket on his holster and held it out. A green beam shot out of the pointed tip, went up and down the man several times, then retracted. "Interesting. He has several compounds in his system which appear to be blocking most neural signals."

"Is it permanent?"

"Negative, I estimate the effects will wear off in thirty minutes."

"It must be Sanford, but why would he bother doing this when he could blow up the entire building from the outside with ease. Why take the risk?"

"Sir, I do not have an answer for you," Atrus said.

"Trisia, would he have taken the risk to gloat?"

Trisia kept watching the building. There were two people walking past, but neither could have been her Father. Cars were sparse this late at night. "I suppose, if he thought he had the advantage."

"But with people froze like this, it will draw attention. And how would he do it without every alarm in Moscow being raised?"

Red's eyes went wide. "James! The cloaking system he developed. Do you think he could have used it?"

"I doubt it. I mean he could have, but the last time he did he got lost in another dimension. He might take risks, but I doubt this is one of them."

"I agree," Trisia said.

"But he could he have fixed the problem?" Red said.

"Doc would know," James said.

"I suppose we can contact him now, we are now past when we left him."

Trisia thought for a moment. "I may not know as much as Keleeigan, but I did rescue him from that dimension. And I saw his designs. I suppose it is possible, but he would need a lot more power than he had previously for one thing."

"Which he has in spades now," Red said. "And I bet he knew what went wrong and fixed it before we saw him."

"Makes sense," James said, looking at the man still frozen

in front of him, "you two had better get in here. I will stay and watch for anything unusual."

A two seconds later he felt a breeze, and Red was standing next to him. "Whoa! Don't do that!"

Red smiled. "Well, you did say to get in here. Besides, these guys aren't going to say anything." Red waved her hand in front of the man's face. "And would you mind dropping the cloak? It would be nice to see who I am talking with."

"Oh right. Atrus, kill the hologram." The area around James flickered and he appeared. "Thanks for not running over me. How did you know I wasn't somewhere else?"

"If you remember, you told me. This was the only guy near the door not moving. Although I found three others nearby in the same condition."

Trisia ran in, breathing hard. "Sheesh, this thing is massive. How are we going to find him, especially if he is cloaked?"

"If I may suggest, the infrared signature from before may still be detectable. From what data I have, if it was missing, he would no longer be in this dimension," Atrus said.

"Can you find him using the building's surveillance system?"

"It may be possible, given enough time."

"Time is one thing I don't think we don't have much of. He won't be hanging around once he sets those power cells to explode, if that is his plan," Red said.

"It may take a while to find Sanford, but the power cells should be easy to find. Their composition is quite different from anything else in this building. One moment. I have detected two at opposite ends of the complex," Atrus said. "I should be able to disable the devices if I have direct contact."

"Show us." In front of them a three-dimensional image appeared of the building with two arrows in opposite corners.

"Red, Trisia you take those two. I have a hunch Sanford has a third one on the top floor," James said.

Red looked at him. "Why?"

"Because it is where the director's office is. And I suspect if he is in the gloating mood, he wouldn't pass up the opportunity."

"But how is Atrus going to disable these two if he is with you?" Trisia said.

"I can remotely through your A.T.E. earpiece," Atrus said.

"Go!" James said as he ran off for the elevators.

Red ran to the one end of the building dodging frozen men at their stations, several locked doors, and a partially operating sensor system which proved to be easier run through before it could detect her instead of having Atrus deactivate it. She reached the power cell and touched her earpiece. "Atrus, what do I do?"

"Take the earpiece out and touch it to the top of the power cell for several seconds."

Red took it out, touched it to the top of the power cell. A few seconds later the device's glow diminished, and went out. She put the earpiece back in. "That's one."

"What I would do for a golf cart about now," Trisia said breathing hard, "this place is huge."

"You want me to do it?" Red asked.

"No, I'm almost there." She approached another door, which unlocked a second before she reached it. "Thanks Atrus."

"Welcome."

She ran through several more corridors and spotted the power cell next to a wall out in the open. Its glow was apparent even from this distance. She wondered why her Father hadn't tried to hide it, but then she realized of course he wouldn't. For his revenge he would make sure everyone would see what he did. "Okay, I am there. So I just take this thing out of my ear and touch it to the power cell?"

"Correct."

Trisia touched the two devices, and a few seconds later the glow disappeared. She placed the A.T.E. back in her ear. "Done. What's next?"

James continued running for the director's office. Along the different checkpoints were guards either frozen at their desks or standing in place motionless. As he reached the office, he paused assuming the door would be secured, but it appeared unlocked. "He must have been here too," he muttered and slipped inside. A man was sitting behind a desk, watching a screen, but not moving. James was about to take another step when the door on the far end of the room opened and Sanford stepped through!

James ducked behind the desk and peered around the corner. Sanford looked around, paused to open the bag slung over his shoulder, removed a power cell, sat it on the floor by the door he just exited, and zipped the bag shut. He tapped the keypad on the top of the device and it began to emanate a bright blue glow.

"James?" Red called. "Are you there?"

No response.

"Trisia? Do you hear me?"

"Sure do. It's not the earpieces."

"Sanford is here and James cannot communicate without giving away our position," Atrus said.

"Dang it! I'll be right there," Red said.

James watched as Sanford stood back up. He pulled the gun from his holster but couldn't get a decent shot from his current position. Especially not so close to power cell. If a stray beam struck it, who knows what could happen. James stood up and pointed the weapon at Sanford. "Sanford! Give it up! Your plan won't work!"

Sanford spun around. "Well … well. You found me, and so fast. I give you credit."

"Give it up. If you move, I will kill you."

"Ah but if you do that, you will also die when this whole area is destroyed. I am the only one who knows how to disable them."

"Oh, you think so? Atrus, show the man." A hologram showed two power cells in their powered down state. Trisia standing near one of them. "As you can see, we disabled those. Care to try again?" The hologram shrank to a point and vanished.

Sanford smiled. "If you could fire the weapon, you would have by now. I suspect you are worried it might trigger the device at my feet. That means you have nothing." The timer on the top of the device continued to tick down. Fewer than ten seconds remained.

"Or I wait and we both die. And I'm sure you don't want that." James' finger tightened on the trigger, trying to decide if the risk was worth it.

"I won't die here. You forget about my ace in the hole." He touched a button on his chest device as he turned towards his left. A beam shot out of the device and the area two feet away flickered as sparks coalesced, creating a green warp of a rough oval shape. Sanford waved. "I bid you adieu."

He dove into the warp and disappeared. The warp itself began to shrink.

James ran over to the power cell as its lights continued to glow brighter. The timer showed five seconds left. He grabbed the device and threw it into the warp a second before it sealed.

Red ran into the room. "Where is he?"

"Gone."

"And the power cell?"

James smiled. "I threw it in after him. I suspect he didn't think I could move that fast."

Red's eyes went wide. "You what?"

"Oh, I'm sure we will find out where he went. Well, once we hear of a gigantic explosion anyway."

"I hope it doesn't detonate inside the warp. While they are different from mine, I still have no idea what the effect it will be."

"He will have to drop the package somewhere. I am sure he couldn't survive inside the warp when it explodes."

"Are you sure?"

"Well, even if it isn't true, he won't take the chance. I'm certain of that."

"I agree," Trisia said, her voice coming through their earpieces, "now can we get out of here? I don't want to be around here when these guys start to move."

"We will be right down." He looked at Red. "Think you can get us back to Doc's?"

"If you can find me a space big enough to run."

James smiled. "Consider it done."

— 12 —

The late afternoon sun dipped behind the trees of Keleeigan's yard when he felt rather than heard the warp as it rippled into existence and expand. He looked out his bedroom window, decided the shower would have to wait, threw on his dirty pants, shoes, and ran down the steps. He got outside the door just as Red emerged from the warp, the last of the three, landing on the grass. The warp slammed shut as usual.

"What happened? I expected to hear from you before now," Keleeigan said.

James stood up first. "We ran into issues."

"What kind of 'issues'?"

"How about Sanford fixed his cloak and used it!" Red said, waving her arms.

"But how could he avoid the toxic side effects?"

"While we don't know if it's safe or not, it looks like he is using one of the power cells to boost its efficiency combined with modifications he learned either from Atrus or his previous experience," James said.

"I assumed you still stopped him?"

"Sure, but he slipped away with most of the power cells." James handed him a bag with two of Sanford's power cells.

Keleeigan looked at it and blinked. "How?"

Red glared at James, and his stance shifted. "Let's say he got lucky. He was standing near one of the power cells as it was building an overload. And I didn't want to trigger it by accident by firing on him."

Keleeigan rubbed his chin, his eyes staring into space as thoughts ran through his mind. "While not a big possibility, it is not zero either. I suppose it could have happened, depending on the current energy charge, the changes he made, and how close to critical mass it is."

James turned towards Red. "See? I made the right call."

"But what do we do now?" Trisia asked, finally standing up while rubbing her hip. She made a mental note to get padded pants next time she traveled with Red. "I mean, we don't know where he will strike next. And before you ask, no I don't have any idea."

Atrus appeared before them. "You could have asked me. I have completed my analysis of Sanford's warp. His exit point appeared in Yellowstone National park."

James cocked his head. "What in the world would he be doing there?"

"I don't know, but it can't be good," Red said.

Professor Keleeigan's eyes flashed. "No, he wouldn't try something so crazy even in his current state."

"Doc? What do you mean?"

"It is too crazy even for him. Forget I said anything."

"Doc, we are talking about the man who tried to blow up Lubyanka Square!"

Keleeigan blew out a breath. "You have a point. Okay, here it is: Yellow Stone is at its core, a giant volcano. If he detonated enough devices in the center, it could be very bad."

James head tilted. "Define bad."

"Well–"

Atrus raised his hand. "If I may, the Yellowstone caldera is one of the largest in the world. If there is sufficient magma in the lower chamber, and if the pressure containing it were suddenly released–"

"The whole thing blows its top?"

"I would not put it in those words, but in essence, yes. As Professor Keleeigan said, 'It would be bad,'" Atrus said before his hologram disappeared.

"No kidding." He turned towards Red. "Can you get us there?"

Red nodded. "I can. As I told you, the temporal warps are what drain me."

Trisia looked at her. "But we arrived before we left last time. Didn't it drain you?"

Red turned. "It did a little. But it was a tiny jump compared to what I am capable of. And I did have almost a day to recover." Red walked over to the center of the Keleeigan's back yard and lowered herself into a sprinting position. "Get ready." She bolted running fast.

Keleeigan retreated back to his house a second before a lighting bolt struck the center and a glowing crack appeared. Red increased her speed and it widened large enough for a human to pass through. "GO! Now!"

Trisia ran for it, James following with Red right behind him. The warp slammed shut with Keleeigan watching, wondering if Linus could actually be planning on triggering something that could affect the entire world.

Green arc's of energy flashed, coalesced into a point, and expanded into a green swirling mass of energy. Linus Sanford stepped through onto the grassy plain. The warp began to shrink behind him and he took a step when something bounced off his leg. He spun around to see the device he had left with the meddlesome man in Russia now on the ground next to him! He dove for it quickly entering the deactivation code. The panel blinked several times before the device's blue glow diminished.

Sanford let out a deep breath and picked up the eight-inch-square device. No damage present. He unshouldered his bag, slipped the device into it, and hoisted the bag back up. "They will pay for destroying my plans. They will all pay."

Near the center of Yellowstone a green torrent of energy appeared. It shimmered, flashed, and flickered several times before a man stepped through. Sanford took a deep breath, and smiled. *They will regret their interference. They all will.*

He continued walking past a sign that read "Norris Geyser Basin". Nearby steam vented, and bubbles peculated up through thick liquid in slow motion. He turned left and right. He only saw one man on the walkway on the far side. The man looked up but paid him no mind. Sanford looked like any other tourist with his jacket, pants, and large bag slung over his shoulder.

He kept walking and neared the Sunday Geyser. He stepped off of the boardwalk, reached into his bag, pulled out a device and attached it under one of the sport columns of the boardwalk. He stepped back onto the boardwalk and looked around. No one had seen him and he continued on.

After a bit of hiking he reached another location of violent spouting water. A sign nearby read "Whirling Geyser" and he placed another device under the boardwalk. A couple noticed his activity and approached. "You know they say not to step off the boardwalk."

Sanford smiled. "Indeed, but I'm an inspector. Have to make sure the posts are not deteriorating. In this kind of climate, it happens more often than we would like."

The man pointed. "I take it this is some kind of monitoring device?"

"You bet. I can monitor everything from my office."

"Ah, well, we won't keep you. Thank you for keeping us safe."

"Of course." Sanford headed north. Two down, and several more to go.

Lightning struck and a flashing red streak of concentrated energy fluctuated before it expanded upon the grassy plain. James fell out of the warp, followed by Trisia and Red. Red landed on her feet. James and Trisia glared. "What? It is not my fault you two can't land on your feet."

Neither one said a word, but they exchanged several looks. Around them nothing could be seen except grass, trees, and a herd of bison in the distance. "Um, Atrus?" Red said.

Atrus appeared in front of them. "Yes, Red?"

"Where are we?"

"Yellowstone National Park, at the coordinates I gave you."

"I know that, but I don't see Sanford. Heck, I don't see anyone. Are you sure this is his target?"

"I am certain he arrived. Now if he stayed, that I cannot answer. As I have said before, I can only detect his exit location if I am able to scan at the point of origin."

"In other words, he was here and went somewhere else."

"It is very possible," Atrus said before he disappeared.

"I would say it is more than possible considering there is nothing here."

Atrus appeared again. "I would not say nothing. We are inside Yellowstone National Park, Lamar Valley to be more specific, and the whole area is volcanically active. Although, this area is to a lesser degree." His image flickered and disappeared.

Trisia cocked her head. "Is he always like that?"

Red nodded. "Yes, he loves to correct us."

Atrus' hologram snapped into being. "Perhaps *correct* is a too strong of a term. I would prefer *educate*," Atrus said.

"Atrus?" James said.

"Yes, Sir?"

"Put a sock in it."

"Acknowledged." He bowed as his hologram shimmered and disappeared.

Red looked around. "If you were a crazed person looking to blow up Yellowstone, where would you go?" Her eyes drifted over to Trisia.

"Don't look at me. I have no idea. I have never been here before."

Atrus appeared before them, but this time his image displayed a sock in his mouth. He mumbled a few unintelligible words.

Red rolled her eyes. "And now you can see he enjoys being a smart-aleck. Atrus, you made your point, take the sock out and tell us what you have found."

The sock disappeared, and Atrus smiled. "It's what you told me to do. And it is not so much as what I have found, but a possible location for Sanford."

They waited several minutes before James broke the silence other than the sound of birds overhead. "Which is?"

An image of the surrounding area appeared next to Atrus. A pulsing dot indicated where they were and to the west a flashing red arrow appeared. "The Norris Geyser Basin. It is the hottest location in Yellowstone for many years to come. Also, of important note, two of the major fault lines in the area intersect at this point."

Trisia cocked her head. "Years to come? How to do you know this?"

Atrus smiled. "I have extensive data on such locations far in the future," Atrus said as both the map and his image vanished.

"We picked him up in the future," Red said.

"But wouldn't it disrupt the natural flow of time you have talked about?"

"No, because the time-line he was in no longer exists."

"But how can that be?"

James sighed. "Let me try."

Red laughed and made a sweeping motion with her hand. "By all means."

"You see there were events set in motion which Sanford triggered causing a global release of nuclear weapons. The resulting wasteland is where we found him. Taking him from that time, since it no longer exists, would not affect anything now or in our future." He turned towards Red. "How's that?"

"You're improving," Red said.

James rubbed shoulders with her. "I had a good teacher."

"But doesn't that mean he would cease to exist?" Trisia said.

"Time-travel is hard to understand and even though I

probably understand more than anyone else alive, it still gives me a headache!" Red laughed.

"So then traveling through a warp must mean you go outside time's influences? Yet the results of what you do would remain?"

Red nodded. "Yes. While we are not immune to the influences, we can keep going even if the time-line shifts. Unless something happens like Keleeigan's unstable temporal field threatening to tear everything apart."

Trisia blinked. "It was that bad? I thought it was only us in trouble."

Red shook her head. "No. If we hadn't reached you when we did, the next jump the lighthouse did, could have been fatal. To you, and to the time continuum." Red lowered herself into a sprinting position. "Time to go." She began running faster and faster clockwise. The air began to swirl. Bison grazing in the distance saw the fast movement and ran in the opposite direction.

Lighting struck and a red flickering crack opened as ozone filled the air. Red increased her speed again, and the crack ripped open. "Now!" she shouted.

Trisia and James ran and dove into the warp with Red half a second behind them. The warp slammed shut with a thunderous clap. Two people peered out from behind a distant tree. "Tell me you got that!" The woman said to the man holding a camera with a long telephoto lens standing near her.

"Umm, er, no."

"What! Why not?"

"Well … " He pointed to the digital readout on the back of the camera. It showed the memory was full.

She smacked the back of his head with her hand. "Idiot! We had the find of a lifetime and you blow it."

"Hey you were the one that said take more pictures than we need, we can always delete them later. And you told me to take all those pictures of the baby bison."

"But you didn't have to do it!"

The man smiled. "Er, perhaps not, but I know where I would have been sleeping if I didn't."

"Men!" the women harrumphed as she headed down the trail leading back to their car.

— 13 —

With a deafening crack, the air split apart revealing a torrent of energy flickering between red and black. The area widened and James leaped out of the warp. He hopped to the side as the other two women exited and the warp slammed shut behind them.

Steam wafted through the air, limiting visibility to only a few feet. Sulfur hung thick in the air and stung their eyes. "I think we are off the path," James choked.

Red held her elbow over her nose. "Naturally we are, you didn't want me to land in the middle of the visitor's center did you?"

"No, but I didn't expect to land in the middle of a geyser."

"Will you two shut it, I think I see a walkway over there," Trisia pointed.

They nodded and made their way towards the wooden structure they could just make out between the clouds of vapor. After several yards the air cleared and they could see the whole boardwalk and several signs past it.

A man approached wearing olive green pants and a khaki shirt. The sunlight glinted off of his badge. "What were you doing off the boardwalk? You realize it is there for a reason. You could have got yourselves killed."

James stepped forward. "Yes," he leaned forward to read the name, "Ranger Dotaten." James pulled his wallet from his pocket and flipped it open. "I am Agent Moknkin, these ladies are with me. Trust me when I say we know all about the boardwalks."

The ranger stiffened. "Without a doubt, Agent Moknkin. Is there something I should know? I mean, the FBI is rarely out here."

James flipped his wallet closed and placed it back inside his jacket pocket. "Nothing at this time. If that changes, I will let you know. And for the moment, it would be best if you did not mention seeing us."

The ranger nodded and smiled. "See who?" He turned on his heel and headed off in the opposite direction.

"That was close," Trisia said.

"Nah, not when I have my get-out-of-trouble-free card," James said with a smirk.

"I wish you would stop doing that. It draws unneeded attention," Red said.

James turned. "What did you want me to do? Shoot him? He was about to write us a ticket, if not worse. Atrus? Any suggestions where to go?"

Atrus appeared before them with a holographic map to his right. "Yes, if you take the west path, there are many geysers ahead. They would be ideal locations." Both flickered, shrunk to a point, and disappeared.

"You heard the man, time for a short walk."

They headed down the western path. The trees grew thicker, then thinned as they continued. Heat radiated from the nearest feature, a deep crater with a deep pool of greyish water. James checked the nearby sign, which read 'Hurricane Vent'. "Atrus? Anything in the area?"

"Negative. But Hurricane Vent is no longer an active Geyser. While it might generate an effect from here, it would be much less pronounced compared to others. Even with the destructive abilities the modified power cells are capable of."

Several people walked past, and James smiled. After they passed he pulled out the Shell and activated it. "Atrus do you have control?"

"Yes, and all systems are functional. What do you wish me to do?"

"I think it is best if we divide in conquer. Activate the cloak and send it on ahead. If I remember from your map, most of the geysers are off to the north. We need to know where he is, and perhaps we can get the drop on him."

"Understood." The Shell hovered out of James' hand and vanished.

"That thing is unreal," Trisia said.

"Yeah, it is pretty cool," James said.

Red rolled her eyes. "Boys and their toys."

"But Miss Red, I am not a toy," Atrus said.

"Atrus! What did I tell you about calling me that? It is Red, just Red, not Miss, not my lady, just Red. Got it?"

"Sorry Red. It was a slip of the tongue."

Trisia's head cocked to one side. "But you don't have a tongue."

"I . . . never mind."

"Good choice," James said.

They continued along the path and while Red offered to run on ahead; they agreed she should conserve her energy should they need it later.

"Sir?" Atrus whispered. "I have located Sanford. He is near Whale's Mouth."

"What? That is a hot spring, not a Geyser. Are you sure?"

"Yes. I can display an image if you wish."

"Not necessary. Is he staying or moving fast?"

"Moving fast on a southern route."

"It doesn't make sense. Why would he be over there?" Red said.

"Unless he already planted his devices," James said.

"Then why would he be hanging around?"

They looked at Trisia who held both her hands waving in front. "Don't look at me. I have no clue why he would do that. I would have thought he would take off. Unless …"

"Unless what?"

"Unless he hasn't finished placing them."

James' eyes flashed. "Atrus? Where does that path go? Does it end up by more geysers?"

"Yes, it loops around back towards us and the Ledge Geyser."

"Okay, you keep a close eye on him. I'm going to the geyser, perhaps head him off."

Red glared at him. "And what are we going to do?"

"Continue looking for the power cells. If we are right and he has placed several of them, time is running out," James said.

"Yes, you're right. Okay, I will take Pinwheel, I remember from Atrus' map it is the farthest from us. Trisia you check out Whirligig Geyser."

They separated, running to their different destinations. A few minutes later James heard Trisia in his ear. "I'm there, but I don't see anything."

James continued running. "Is the boardwalk flush with the ground? If not look under it," James said between breaths.

Trisia looked around but didn't see a ranger. She stepped off of the boardwalk into the mushy ground and looked under the supports closest to the geyser. By the far edge she saw a small glowing device attached to the support. "Got one."

"Disable it like before. I'm almost there."

Trisia removed her earpiece and touched it to the device. But the power cells' glow didn't diminish. She put the earpiece back in. "Umm, we may have a problem. It didn't shut down."

"What?"

"I found three, and none of them shut down like the ones in Moscow. He must have changed something," Red said.

"Affirmative. I have detected a change in the circuitry. There is now an encrypting system added to the controller. I will have access in a few moments," Atrus said.

James arrived at the Ledge Geyser. Sanford wasn't anywhere to be seen. "Atrus, how close is Sanford?"

"You will see him in 1.5 minutes," Atrus replied.

James ran for a line of trees hiding the loop of approaching path. Several seconds later, right in time with Atrus' warning, Sanford came into view. He continued along at a fast pace.

A slight beep emanated from their earpieces. "I have determined the encryption. Red, Trisia, if you touch the earpiece again to the devices I will be able to shut them down," Atrus said.

Red and Trisia touched the glowing devices in almost perfect sync. The glow on the first set of devices shut down. Red proceeded with the next. "Mine's done. I am surprised there weren't more," Trisia said.

"Atrus, do you still have him?"

"Yes, he has stopped on the boardwalk, closest to the geyser."

"Good, we can't risk him placing more. Take him out."

"I regret to inform you, he still has several devices in his bag. I am uncertain the modifications he has made will tolerate an energy discharge of that nature. It may set them off."

"Dang it, I forgot about that. Activate my hologram then, cloak me. We will need to do it the 'old-fashioned' way."

James disappeared and began walking towards Sanford. "I fail to see how this is 'old-fashioned' considering no one has done it before," Atrus whispered.

"Atrus, stick a sock in it," James whispered.

By the time he got close to Sanford, he had placed two more devices and continued down the boardwalk. James was almost upon him when the wind changed and a vapor cloud blew directly over them. James thought nothing of it until Sanford's eyes went wide, hit a button on his belt and disappeared.

"What happened? How did he see me?"

"The vapor cloud's image changed too quickly to simulate. A slight variation in your image revealed your outline to him," Atrus stated.

"Indeed. You really should build a better cloaking system," Sanford called.

James moved in a different direction, then changed again. If Sanford was planning on attacking, he wouldn't know where. "Oh, I don't know. I think it works well."

"Not as well as mine!" Sanford said. The voice echoed and James couldn't tell where it was coming from.

"If you say so."

"I do. Now, if you will excuse me, I must be going."

"So soon? Even before all the volcanic action starts?"

"Ah so you figured out what I am doing here? Very good, but not entirely surprising."

"Then why don't you give up? You can't win."

"Oh, can't I? I have already won."

"You have? I don't see a volcano spewing lava or ash, do you?"

"No, but it will soon enough. I have devices set up all over. You won't be able to get to them in time. And one will be enough."

"He is correct, one of them will trigger an event," Atrus said in James' ear.

James stiffened and gave a hidden smile. "One might be enough, but we found them all and deactivated them."

"I doubt that. I added protections to this batch."

"Oh you mean that little encryption? Atrus cracked it in a minute flat."

"So you took the bait. Excellent."

James blinked. "Bait?"

"I set them up if the encryption system deactivated the timers would resume after fifteen minutes. Enough time so you would think it disabled them, only to come back and kill you."

"Why are you telling me this?"

"Because you can't stop them, that's why."

A green oval appeared at the edge of the boardwalk. "I bid you adieu. Give my regards to … well … God." The green sheen of the warp rippled as if a stone was thrown into a green pool, then slammed shut.

James ran over to the glowing power cells. "Atrus disable the cloak and deactivate these." He pulled Atrus' cylinder from the holster under his arm and touched it to the first of the power cells. The glow faded and went out. "The first one is disabled, please move onto the next."

"Red, Trisia, anything from your power cells?"

"Nope, why?" Red said.

"Yes," Trisia said, "I was about to call you, mine started glowing again."

"Touch your earpiece to it again," Atrus said.

Trisia did so, but the glow didn't diminish this time. "I tried, but it is still on."

"Yes, it would appear the encryption system was not the only controlling force on these devices. I am scanning to find the solution." A green beam reached out from the cylinder in James' hand and ran over the nearest power cell horizontally several times before retracting. "It is quite curious, I am not sure how he accomplished this."

"There must be a way," Trisia said. "He would not have a way to turn them off. He would never trust them 100% without some sort of backup shut down."

"Ah, I think I have found it. Touch your earpiece to it again," Atrus said.

"That did it, the glow is diminishing," Trisia said.

"I'm doing the same with mine as they come back on. The first one just did," Red said.

"Umm Atrus, what about these?" James asked, pointing to the devices at his feet.

"We have to wait until they activate, then we can change them permanently."

"What did you do?"

"It is quite simple. Sanford changed the power down sequence to activate a delay timer. After several minutes they would reactivate, and either detonate or resume the countdown depending on how long they had been offline for."

"And how did you fix it?"

"I have locked the timer into a continuous loop. If

reactivated, they will shut down again a few seconds later. It will endure until we dismantle them."

"Good, glad I brought a larger bag in my pack," James said as he removed his backpack and pulled out a bag that expanded to the size they needed. "Glad I decided on picking one of these up." He grabbed the device at his feet to place in the bag, but it started glowing. "Umm, Atrus? Are you sure about that loop?"

"Yes," Atrus said, and a moment later the glow dissipated. "I told you it will remain in the loop until we dismantle them."

"Red, Trisia? Meet you near the Hurricane Vent."

"I don't want to carry these power cells. I don't care if they are in a continual loop. Their repeating glowing cycle has me worried," Red said.

"I agree. I'm a little leery of carrying these things. I mean who knows what my Father did to them," Trisia said over the earpiece.

"I have scanned the devices, and they will not detonate. I would not have you carrying them if there was the slightest chance of a failure," Atrus said.

"Atrus, we all would feel better if they hardware disabled."

"Very well. If you open the side, there is a release. Flipping it will allow removal of the top section."

James took the device back out of his bag and set it on the ground next to the other power cell. He looked at the side but didn't see a way to open them. "Atrus, I don't see a way to open the side."

"Me either," Trisia said.

"There are two small holes. One of your standard Philips-head screwdrivers should be able to remove the two fasteners that are holding the side in place," Atrus said.

"Slight problem there, I don't have one," Red said.

Trisia felt her pockets. "Nope, no screwdriver."

James fished in his pocket and pulled out a multi-tool knife. Looking over it, he found the screwdriver and flipped it out. "I hope this is long enough," he muttered. Inserting the tool into the small hole, it reached the screw a millimeter before the housing of the knife bumped into the power cells' casing. "I think it is long enough. I am turning the first screw." He twisted the little knife several times and the magnetic head pulled the screw out of the hole. James repeated it for the other screws. "Screws removed, I am removing the side covers." He opened the covers and found the releases. He flipped them and the top housing lifted off with ease. "Now what?"

Red ran up to him. "Give me that knife! I'm sitting on three of these things!" James held it out and Red grabbed it. "Thanks." James blinked, and she was gone.

"It still amazes me when I see her do that. Atrus, what's next?"

"Inside you will find several plug-in circuit boards. Remove the third one from the side with the screw holes. However, do not touch the first or second. It could cause issues if you do."

"Right," James said as he started to pull the board.

"One warning, do not pull the board when the device is enabled, or glowing."

James stopped as the device's sides began to glow again. "Geeze Atrus, could you have told me before I started pulling on the thing?"

"You didn't start yet, you only had your hand on the proper circuit card," Atrus said.

"I got them open and pulled the cards. Anything else, Atrus?" Red said.

"No, without that card the devices cannot generate or otherwise utilize power."

"Umm guys, I hate to say this but a crowd has gathered, and a ranger is approaching. It's not the same guy we ran into before. What do I do?"

James stuffed the cards in his bag, put the top housing back on the power cells, and placed them in his bag as well. "Tell them Agent Moknkin will be there in a minute to explain the situation," James said as he ran for the Sunday Geyser. When he reached Trisia, a large crowd stood on the boardwalk and the ranger was trying to move them along. But apparently the look of a strange device at the feet of a young woman was too much for their curiosity.

James fought to catch his breath. "Is there a problem?"

The ranger looked up and down James' suit, pausing at the bags slung over his shoulder. "Who are you?"

James reached into his pocket, pulled out his wallet and with a deft motion flipped it open. "I am Agent Moknkin. I repeat, is there a problem?"

The ranger looked at James' badge and stiffened. "Yes sir, this woman is very suspicious and has an odd box at her feet. I feared it was a bomb and I am in the process of clearing tourists. I have called for assistance."

James nodded. "That is proper protocol, however, this woman is with me. There was a threat, but we have neutralized it. Continue clearing the tourists from this area and you are not under any circumstances to reveal the true nature of what you have heard to anyone. Is that understood?"

"Yes, Sir I do."

"Good and tell those that respond to your call the same thing." The ranger nodded as James took several steps and stood next to Trisia.

"Thanks," she said out the corner of her mouth, "I don't know what they would have done if you hadn't showed up."

"Probably nothing, that is protocol. At least until a bomb squad from the Department of Homeland Security arrived. It would take a little while though. Still, it would have been a problem."

"No kidding. Now how about that screwdriver, so I can take the top off of this thing?" She held out her hand.

"I don't have it. Didn't you hear Red? She took it."

"Must have been when the ranger arrived."

James blinked, and Red was standing next to him. He jumped. "Don't do *that!* What if someone saw you?"

Red smiled. "They would think they were seeing things. Here." She placed the knife in his hands, one of the power cells in his bag, and another one in his other hand. "There, I will be back in a minute."

He blinked again, and she was gone. "How does one ever get used to that?" Trisia said.

"I haven't and I have been with her a lot longer than you." He handed her the knife. "Get the cover off of that thing. The sooner we leave the better," James said as he placed the power cell Red had given him into the bag.

"No kidding," Trisia said. She removed the two screws, flipped the release, took off the cover, pulled the board, and replaced the cover. "Scratch one more." She picked up the power cell and slipped it into the bag slung over James' shoulder. "Now can we get out of here?"

"In another second or two, if I'm right." Red appeared standing next to James again holding the last of the devices.

"Thought so." She placed it in his bag, and they headed south down the boardwalk away from the larger crowds of people.

They hustled down the path and turned off on a side route, heading away from the geyser basin and towards the forest. After twenty minutes of hiking, they arrived at a clearing, surrounded by trees. Red felt the ground. "This spot looks as good as any." She walked towards the edge of the clearing. "Get ready." She lowered herself into a sprinter's position and bolted running. The air swirled around James and Trisia. They moved off from the center to allow room for what was to come.

Red increased her speed again and clouds rolled in. Electric discharges went back and forth between them. Red pushed and a bolt shot to the center of the clearing leaving a crack in its wake. The crack fluctuated, shrank, then grew three times its original size as Red forced it open. The rip shrank again.

"What's wrong?" Trisia shouted, trying to be heard over the storm surrounding them.

"She's tired. I was afraid of this, she did too much back and forth running earlier."

"Anything we can do?"

James shook his head. "Nope, it is up to her."

She gave another burst of speed, expanding the rip into a full warp. "Will ... you ... two ... shut ... up ... and ... JUMP!"

They ran across the soft grass, jumping into the red and black portal in space and time. Trisia entered first and disappeared, followed by James with Red half a second behind him.

Inside the warp, James could feel Red straining to point them in the right direction. He reached back, grabbed her hand, and focused his mind to join her forcing an exit point.

We have to get to Doc. He felt something flow over his hands and quickly engulfed the rest of this body.

James crashed out of the warp and turned back to grab Red as she fell out into his arms. Trisia managed to get out a microsecond before the warp sealed itself with a thunderous crash.

"That didn't feel like the others. And how did you get out ahead of me?" Trisia said.

"I know, I had to help her. Red? You okay?"

"Mmm … so … tired … must … rest." She fell asleep in his arms. James turned, slid his other arm down under her legs, and swept her off of her feet in a smooth motion.

James pointed his head towards Keleeigan's patio door. "Will you stop standing there looking at us and open the door!"

"Oh! Sorry!" Trisia ran over to open it but instead bumped into Keleeigan as he slid one of the doors open and stepped out.

"What happened? Is Red okay?" Keleeigan said.

James carried her through the doors without a word and headed over to the living room with its large couch. He lay Red down and flicked the red hair from her face. "She will be in time."

"I don't understand, she didn't get this tired last time," Keleeigan said.

"No. The problem is she has been warping us all over with little rest in between. Granted, non-temporal warps don't drain her that much, but they add up. Coupled with using her speed to travel between geysers, it was too much."

Keleeigan nodded. "I see. I assume you were successful?"

James handed him the bag of power cells. "You could say that."

Keleeigan gazed inside the bag. "He tried to use this many? One would have done it. Although, they are much smaller than my original design. I suppose it is possible more might be needed. But two would have been enough, I'm sure."

James shrugged. "He is all about overkill now. And we have no idea where he will strike next. Atrus, have you found his latest exit point?"

"Yes, he went back to Alaska, almost the same location he did before."

"Hmm back to his old lab? That could be a problem."

Trisia smiled. "I don't think so."

James turned. "Why not?"

"Because I triggered his processing cores to explode like he did to mine before we left. There isn't anything left for him to use."

Keleeigan smiled. "Smart girl."

She smiled back. "I try."

"He used up most of his power cells and doesn't have a lab to make more, which makes them a rare commodity he will have to be more careful with. That should give us some time. At least enough for Red to get back on her feet. Now if we can just find out what his next move is."

14

At the end of a dead-end street the air swirled a microsecond before it ripped apart revealing a green mass of coalesced energy from another dimension. The energy varied from intense green to a lime green, to a yellow green before it flickered red and back to the dark green again. Sanford emerged from the dimensional portal and checked his surroundings for a few seconds before the portal shrank to a point, disappearing behind him.

Again, they tracked and stopped me! Sanford walked out of the space between the restaurant and a clothing store. People passed him along the sidewalk, but none of them gave him a second look. He kept walking towards the edge of town, and to his lab.

Twenty minutes later he reached the elevator to his lab, but it wouldn't respond to his touch or code. Sanford cocked his head and pried the doors apart with a broken piece of rebar, revealing the emergency ladder cut into the side of the elevator shaft. He dropped the rebar into the shaft, reached over, grabbed the closest rung, and began the long decent. Several times his footing slipped, leaving him dangling over a hundred-foot drop, but he pulled himself back to the wall with difficulty and his feet back on the rungs.

He continued down and after several more near accidents; he reached his lab. The elevator car sat dead beneath his feet, and the emergency access hatch refused to open. He grabbed the rebar, jammed it into the hatch hinges. After several attempts the hinges gave way, sending the hatch door flying off to the side, where it hit the shaft wall, and bounced back onto the elevator's roof. He shimmied inside the narrow opening and with more help of the rusted steel bar, pried the doors open.

The lab was not as he left it. Acrid fumes wafted through the crack in the doors stinging his nose and eyes. Tables were overturned and blackened, the large screens on the walls were cracked with their edges melted. The processing cores were all black, scorched or melted into a pile of useless goo. Nothing was left. He smiled. *Just want I wanted them to think.* He pried the doors open the rest of the way, exited the elevator, walked over to a blackened wall on the far side of the lab, and slid it back. But his eyes didn't fall on what he expected. Another lab, almost the same size as the one he was in, showed the same destruction. Everything was burnt, blasted, or melted. He had lost both his lab and his backup. *How? How could they have known this existed? Trisia! She must have known I wouldn't have left so easily otherwise.*

Sanford walked over to an overturned chair, pulled it upright, and sat on the ripped padding. For the first time he was without a place to fall back to. He sat with his head in his hands.

He heard a slight beep. At first, he thought he was hearing things. But then he heard it again. And again. He walked over towards the far right corner of the room. He heard it again as he approached. Sanford cocked his head. What could still be functional here? He pulled one of the melted and slagged processing cores free and threw it to the side. He did the same with the second large box, then the third. But the forth didn't show the same damage. Blackened yes, but not melted. And it had a glowing green activity light.

He realized the beep meant it had lost access to its siblings and was alerting him to a connection failure. He disconnected it from the others and its beeping stopped.

Sanford walked over to one of the overturned tables looking for a working keyboard. He flipped several back upright, those that still had legs, to no avail. But along the south wall he found an old keyboard he never used and left in the packaging because of its odd shape. The packaging sat blackened and ripped on one side. But the keyboard itself looked undamaged. *Now for a monitor.* He looked at screen after screen. Every single one of them were ruined. This one had a crack down the middle and its liquid oozed out the edges. Another was missing the connection ports.

He was about to give up when he remembered a screen with a small crack in the corner, and he had put it on the floor facing the wall, under one table. The crack was a defect, and he planned on returning it later for a replacement. It might have been spared the worst of the explosion.

Sanford flipped several more tables to reach the wall and found the monitor, its screen still facing the wall. He picked it up and slowly turned it around. The crack had not spread!

Grabbing its power cable, he walked back over to the one remaining core. Plugging in the monitor and keyboard, the screen came to life and showed the core was still running its last task. He instructed it to stop and show the data available.

Sanford smiled when he saw all the data from Trisia's laptop was intact! He began looking through it. There had to be something he could use. Something to give him an edge.

His eyes glanced over something about Keleeigan, but since so much of the data discussed his power cell, he didn't pay it any attention. Then something gnawed at the back of his mind. He scrolled back. It was a map to a location in the middle of nowhere. Far from any normal roads. "What in the world could this be?" he muttered. "Whatever it is, it has to be very significant."

Sanford punched in the coordinates into the device strapped to his chest, powered down the core, disconnected it, and tucked it under his arm. He pushed another button and the air in front of him rippled energy coalesced into an oval green shape along the wall. He smiled, hopped into it, and disappeared.

A green rip opened over a grassy area and Sanford stepped through. The green warp slammed shut behind him with a *bang*. He looked around but saw nothing. Then he felt a slight depression with his toe. Digging into the grass, he found metal.

Metal? Here? It's Keleeigan's lab! Trisia told me she worked with him for over a year so she must have had access. But how to get down there. There had to be a key or something, but there wasn't any mention of it on the map he had found.

Then an idea hit him. He had never done it without knowing the exact coordinates before, but perhaps he could get close. Doing the math in his head, he entered another set of coordinates, very similar to the previous ones except adjusted down and to his right.

He pushed a button on the device on his chest and three beams shot out of the front as they swirled around for a second before joining at the center. Once they combined the resulting wash of energy shot forward and opened the shimmering green oval shaped energy mass. Sanford smiled and stepped into it.

He floated for a second, then felt himself fall out and land with a crash up on a solid concrete floor. He rubbed his leg. He hadn't broken it, but it sure hurt. He blinked in the dark. There were a few dim lights, and most of them flickering, but not enough to see where he was. He reached into the bag slung over his shoulder and pulled out a flashlight. He looked up in time to see the green warp slam shut. He was lucky. A few degrees different either way and he would have either broken his leg, or materialized half inside the ceiling or a wall.

He checked the device on his chest; the dimensional door's status lights all showed green, except for power. He checked the details and frowned. It would be several hours before the system recharged enough to generate another portal.

Around him tables sat with a variety of equipment. Some of it in the middle of construction. Others appeared to be only spare parts. The big screen attached to one wall sat dark and brooding. Several rectangular devices continued to run, their lights flickering. Computational cores, he assumed.

Sanford stood and winced as pain shot up his leg. No alarms had been triggered at his entrance. *Must be Moris didn't expect anyone to enter his lab without breaking something.* He spotted two cameras in opposite corners of the room, but they sat in a powered-down state.

He sat the bag down on one table and pulled out one of his power cells. He still had three left. Slipping a strap over his forehead, he attached the small flashlight and began removing the cover of one of the power cells. He made several adjustments and connected it to the device on his chest. A second later the power indicator blinked full. He disconnected it, reached into his bag, pulled out the core from his lab, sat it on the table, connected the core to the power cell. Energy flowed into the core and its, and the tiny status lights came alive.

Sanford grabbed a keyboard, mouse and monitor from one of several on the tables around him and connected them to the core. The screen flickered, flashed and showed the core's readiness. He punched in a search and had all the data given to him displayed. He swore as he scrolled through. It was all there, but it wasn't enough.

While the data gave detailed information on inside of the temporal warps he had heard about, there wasn't enough about the creation process. He had assumed it wouldn't be necessary.

Sanford sat in a chair by the table and sighed. *So close, I am so close.* His head popped up. *If Keleeigan generated the temporal warps, his data must be here.* He grabbed a data cable and connected one end to his processing core, and the other end to one of Keleeigan's. Accessing Keleeigan's cores via the attached keyboards would be easier, it would also be the first thing anyone would try. Sanford hoped tunneling in might not be noticed. Or at least not as fast.

The cable gave a stable connection, and Sanford entered through his system. Digging around, he found a few references to a temporal project, but he couldn't break the encryption. At least not without several months and a huge cluster of machines working on it.

Searching the various folders he found one scrap of data which had been thrown away rather than encrypted, but the space it occupied hadn't been overwritten yet. Checking it over several times, he wondered if it was enough. He had the ability to appear anywhere he wished; adding time to it can't be much of a difference.

The formula he found might work, but it could be tricky. And it required a special ionic energy that has been through super heated plasma in addition to the power cell. Something that could, when concentrated, open a temporal rip able to be further expanded if you threw enough energy at it. *Lighting? Could it be that simple?*

Sanford thought about it, and it might work, but to harness a bolt at the precise moment would be difficult. And not fry himself in the process. He flipped several plastic connectors near his shoulders and the device on his chest loosened. He lowered it to the table and got to work.

He connected it to his remaining core and ran several simulated tests. It seemed possible, providing he could add the third component. He flashed the alternate sequence to its memory, disconnect it from the core, and fastened it back to his chest. His eyes narrowed as he tapped out a search command on the keyboard connected to his core. Several red lights flashed as an alarm started screeching in his ear. *Dang it! The system detected me trying to access the most recent logs.*

Sanford stuffed the power cells back into his bag, unplugged his last core, tucked it under his arm, and pressed a button on his chest. Three laser beams shot out, locked on to the wall in front of him, and an energy discharge launched from his chest. The energy landed on target and ripped open a space between dimensions. The green mass of energy swirled, rippled, and expanded as a warp formed. Sanford smiled and stepped through.

15

James looked up at the sound coming from several speakers mounted in the wall of the living room.

"Doc? What is that sound? The screeching is hurting my ears."

Trisia put her hands over her ears. "Mine too."

"Someone's in my lab!" Keleeigan went off like a shot towards the basement door, faster than a man half his age. Trisia and James followed.

As they came down the steps Keleeigan was already on a laptop. "I don't see anyone here," Trisia said.

"Not here! My main lab!" Keleeigan worked quickly trying to get the remote cameras working and activate some sort of countermeasure.

Trisia smiled. "Are you sure? Heck, I know for a fact no one could get in there."

"Yeah Doc, I can't see how anyone could get inside. That place is a literal bunker with more protections than dogs have fleas," James said.

"I know, but somehow it happened. It has to be Sanford."

James shook his head. "No way, he wouldn't know where it is."

They both looked at Trisia. She held up her hands. "Don't look at me. I never told him."

Keleeigan tapped a few more keys and a monitor to his right lit up with a green-tinted image of Sanford stooped over working on his chest-device sitting on one of the tables. "Oh yeah? Then how did he find it?"

"Doc! Do you have any way to stop him?"

"I do. They aren't set up to do so inside the lab, but I will have it in a second." He tapped several more keys when several lights flashed on the screen. "Dang it! When I activated them, it also activated the alarms in the lab. I forgot to disable them."

They watched as Sanford looked up, gathered up the items from the table in front of him and walked towards the far wall. "Doc! Hurry!"

"I know my boy, I know. Just a few more seconds."

They watched helpless as Sanford pushed a button, opened a green warp, and stepped through.

Keleeigan hit the table in front of him with a balled fist. "Dang it! So close!" He stood up, grabbed his keys and headed for the stairs.

"Where are you going?" James said.

"To see what that slime ball was doing in my lab!"

"But can't you find that out remotely?"

"No. At least not everything."

James started following with Trisia right behind him. "Then I am coming too. Who knows, he might have set a trap. If so, you will need backup."

Trisia smiled, peeking around James. "And I'm not staying here. You might need another pair of hands."

Keleeigan sighed. "All right. My car is parked out front."

Keleeigan hopped into the driver's seat with James sitting

next to him and Trisia climbing into the back. He turned the key, gunned the hybrid engine and smiled as he activated the hover system. The car floated up into the air. "We should be there in twenty minutes. I wish Red could have got us there. I hate waiting even that long."

"I know Doc, but she will be out of it for at least the rest of the day."

Trisia looked out at the ground below. "When did you invent this anyway?"

Keleeigan smiled. "When I realized my overdrive system would never be reliable enough. This is much better. Not to mention you don't have to worry about traffic."

James smiled at the passing roads and trees below. "No kidding. It is one sure way to get above it all."

As they neared the lab Keleeigan lowered the car so James could lean out the window with Atrus. A green beam shot out, scanning the landing area and the ground beneath them.

"I do not detect any traps or alterations in the landing area," Atrus said.

"How about the tunnel or the lab itself?" Keleeigan asked.

"I am having difficulty penetrating the shielding. But based on the data I have from the previous visit, the probability of alteration is low."

Keleeigan smiled. "My shielding is better than I thought if you can't penetrate it."

They could hear a slight grunt. "I do have limitations, while they are small, they do exist," Atrus said.

Trisia looked down to the grassy area below. "Now what?"

"We land obviously and see what he did to my lab."

Keleeigan descended until the tires touched down into a specific soft grassy spot. He flipped up a hidden compartment and entered a ten digit number on a keypad attached to the dash. The ground beneath them went down with a jolt, revealing a tunnel twice as large as the car and ending in a door of equal size at the far end. Keleeigan activated the conventional drive and moved the car off of the platform. A second later it went back up, sealing them in.

Keleeigan got out and waved at them. "Well, don't just sit there, come on." They moved along the tunnel. The walls were smooth and arched up at a gentle angle to the ceiling. James knew the half circular design would support a lot more weight than a rectangle.

Upon reaching the door, red light beams shot out from several hidden locations. One beam locked onto each of their heads, while another centered on the middle of their chests. Trisia's eyes went wide. "Umm, shouldn't this system be off when you sent the signal from the car?"

"No. I had this on full lock-down. But I thought no one could get past the door without triggering the alarms, so I never bothered activating the sensors inside. I didn't plan on someone being able to teleport in there."

"Then how did he trigger the alarm?"

"I don't know. That is what we are here to find out. Well, one thing."

"Please enter the access code or termination system will activate," a voice boomed.

"Doc?" James said.

"Improper response. You have one more chance to enter the proper access code or the termination system will activate," the voice boomed.

Keleeigan held a finger to his lips, causing James and Trisia to hold their breath. He leaned over, entered a fifteen digit number on a keypad next to the door, and the beams shut down. He entered another code and the door ground open.

Inside, the lights turned on automatically with the door opening and Keleeigan looked around. "I don't see anything unusual."

James stepped in front of Keleeigan and held his arm across the man's chest. "Wait a sec, I have a better idea." He removed Atrus from the pouch on his holster and held him out. "Atrus, see what you can find."

A green beam shot out going up, down, then back and forth across the entire room. "I do not detect any sort of danger, or entanglement in the area. Little has changed from the last time I was in this room except for the missing equipment migrated from here to Professor Keleeigan's basement. Although I do detect one monitor, keyboard, and mouse out of place." Atrus generated a holographic finger bobbing up and down over the items in question.

"Thanks Atrus. What could he be doing with those? Shouldn't his laptop have them built in, or the equivalent?"

Trisia shook her head. "No, he gave his laptop to me. At least that is what he said. Perhaps he had more, but I don't remember seeing him have a laptop. Unless it was in the bag slung over his shoulder."

"Could have been, but if it was, why would he need a screen and keyboard?" James said.

Keleeigan walked over to the table Atrus was pointing at and held up a data cable. "This should not be here either." His eyes went wide as he remembered the box under Sanford's arm. "He connected something to my system!" Keleeigan ran over to another workstation that still had its monitor and keyboard attached. He typed in his codes and checked the access logs. "Strange, he didn't access my research. I didn't think he could crack my encryption, but he didn't even try!"

James and Trisia walked over and looked at the screen.

"Anything else he could have accessed?" James said.

Keleeigan shook his head. "No. If he had accessed anything it would show access or a digital footprint. Nothing shows a download or even access on the lowest level."

"Doc there must be something. He wasn't in here for the scenery," James said.

"Maybe the alarm went off before he could?" Trisia asked.

"The alarms!" Keleeigan said tapping keys.

"I don't get it," James said.

"If he tripped the alarms, it must be he accessed something. But it must be something I never would've bothered to check." The screen changed, displaying several rows of numbers and file names. Keleeigan pointed at one. "There! He triggered the alarm when he was trying to look at the log. But that doesn't make any sense. Why would he be looking at the access logs? He never got anything in the first place. Changing the logs is something you do to cover your tracks." Keleeigan sat in the nearby chair lab chair with a loud thump.

"That is strange."

Trisia pointed to the keyboard. "Professor, would you mind if I took a look?"

Keleeigan rolled back in the chair and gestured towards the keyboard. Trisia wasted no time and brought up all the logs for every file usage, no matter how slight. Still nothing, then she found a record of a recovery program was activated. "Professor, you didn't run a file recovery program by remote today, did you?"

"Of course not! Why would I have any reason to do that?"

"Well, this is what my Father was up to then. I don't know why, but he was trying to recover data from your system."

"Let me see that." Trisia moved aside as Keleeigan rolled back in front of the screen. "You're right. But he couldn't have found anything, I routinely wipe files rather than a simple delete."

Trisia leaned closer. "But he did see this?" Trisia pointed to one line on the screen indicating one file was recovered. "I don't know what it was, or where he put it after but he did find something."

Keleeigan rubbed his chin. "I can't imagine what he could have found except maybe my grocery list. I shred everything else." He leaned back in his chair. "If he recovered a file, but didn't want me to know he did …hmmm." He sat up with a jolt and his fingers flew across the keyboard as he activated the same file recovery program. A few seconds later it showed one file recovered. "Here it is!" Keleeigan's face went white. "Dang it!"

James leaned over. "What is it Doc?"

"For some reason the temp holding area for the system wasn't wiped properly. It is a partial file showing the early formula I used."

"Doc? What formula?"

Keleeigan turned in his chair. "Time travel. It is a small scrap from my time travel notes."

"Do you think he has enough to create a temporal warp?"

"If it was anyone else, I would say no. But being Sanford has the ability to jump to almost any place, with the proper modifications time travel isn't much of a stretch."

James shuddered as the thought of a madman with the ability to go anywhere in time. "This is not good."

"The only good thing is this data is old. Also, even with his current technology, I doubt he can do it right away. It will take some development."

Trisia sighed. "And he has the ability to do all of this because of me."

Keleeigan stood, placed both hands on the young woman's shoulders and looked into her eyes. "It is not your fault. I know what you were trying to do. I can't think of anyone who wouldn't try to save their parents if they could. And I told you, I would have helped if you asked."

Trisia's eyes fell to the ground. "But you didn't think there was anything to save."

"No, I didn't. But this doesn't mean I wouldn't help you try. You worked with me for almost a year, you should know I would have."

Trisia's eyes watered, and she threw her arms around him. "Oh Professor, I'm so sorry."

Keleeigan squeezed her back. "Hey, what is done is done. I don't blame you. And you can call me Doc. You are the second person I have given that honor to."

James smiled. "Actually the third, although Red didn't want it."

Keleeigan smiled. "Okay, the second person I gave it to, and they accepted."

Trisia let go of Keleeigan. "Thank you."

"You have nothing to thank me for my child. Now shall we see about where Sanford went?"

"Atrus? Anyway we can determine where he went?"

Atrus appeared before them. "I regret to inform you it is not possible. If I had been here sooner, I may have been able to track traces left by passing through dimensions."

"Is there any other way we can track him?"

"I can detect if such a dimensional warp appears in the area. But nothing more."

Trisia dried her eyes and cocked her head. "How about satellites? Can you link to those and find him?"

Atrus turned towards her. "I can access such primitive systems, yes. But it will not be of any substantial use."

James crossed his arms. "Why not? Too far away?"

"Too primitive and too far away."

Keleeigan continued rubbing his chin. "Can you get anything out of them at all?"

"I can access them, and the communications network that powers them 'with my eyes closed' I believe is the phrase."

James smiled. "But you can do anything with your eyes closed."

Atrus' eyes snapped open. "Did I use the phrase incorrectly?"

"Not at all. I was making a joke."

Atrus' eyes narrowed. "I should have known that."

"Wait a sec. If you can access the communications grid, can you monitor it as well?" Trisia asked.

Atrus nodded. "With relative ease."

"Then perhaps you might detect him talking with someone else and trace the call."

"It is possible. But there might be gaps. My power supply is not infinite, and I will need to recharge it soon."

"Try to plan around monitoring daylight hours the most," Trisia said.

"That could be difficult considering it is always daylight somewhere on the planet."

Trisia smiled. "I mean in the USA, I doubt he would go somewhere else."

"What about Russia? He might have more resources there," James said.

"Possible, but I doubt it. I think he is still in this country. He knows it the best, and one often sticks with what they know."

Keleeigan nodded. "Very true. I can't imagine him going somewhere else if he could avoid it."

"Atrus monitor as much as you can, with priority on USA daylight hours. And I hope he is not a night owl," James said.

Keleeigan laughed. "Not a chance. He would work late into the night if he had to, but it was far from his preference."

"Good. All we can do now is wait."

16

The air rippled and swirled as a vortex of energy erupted from the side of a wall. It spread out into a green oval and Sanford stepped out. The green warp slammed behind him.

His coordinates were on target, and he walked out from behind the white building into the empty parking lot. No one had seen him arrive, and he started walking away from the center of town. He passed a sign that said "Welcome to Eastport!" and smiled. *No one will look for me here.* Sanford was certain he had never told Trisia of his time spent here, the name he used, or that he once owned a house on the edge of the town limits long ago.

He needed time, and he was certain to get it here. He continued walking and crossed north several blocks to a small motel. In truth, it was more of an inn, and looked more run-down than he remembered with its aging flaking paint and sagging boards, but he put that out of his mind. He walked in and the bell over the door jingled.

A lady came out from behind a dividing wall that led to a room at the rear of the counter. She had long black hair extending down past her backside and wore simple jeans with too many holes and a shirt with almost as many. The entrance area also showed more dirt than he remembered, and he could smell a slight hint of mustiness in the air. "Can I help you?"

"Yes. I would like a room for a few nights."

The woman nodded. "It's $40 a night. How would you like to pay?"

Sanford thought for a moment. He didn't have his wallet, and even if he did, all of his credit cards had been canceled with the deceleration of his death. He had cash reserves, but he needed Internet access to get to them. He thought about killing her, but that would draw too much attention. And right now he wanted to be as invisible as possible. He smiled his most charismatic smile. "Could you bill me?"

The woman shook her head, making her hair swish back and forth. "No, I'm sorry sir it's against policy."

Sanford continued the smile, not letting it waver until he looked into her eyes, and thought it best if he did. His gaze drifted down, as did his smile. "I understand. I didn't want to tell anyone, but I guess I have to. I lost my wallet, I don't have my car anymore, and I will be wandering the street if you don't let me stay the night. I can pay later on, but I have to get access to my bank," Sanford paused to pat the box under his arm, "once I get online, I can pay you."

The woman eyed him up and down several times. "I may regret this, but okay I will let you stay TONIGHT only. If you haven't paid by tomorrow afternoon, I will kick you out no matter the sob story. Got it?"

Sanford nodded. "I understand. Thank you, you have saved me."

"Maybe, maybe not. Either way, you had better give me the cash tomorrow or else." She handed over a key and pointed to the steps to her left. "Room Two, upstairs on the left."

Sanford took several steps, placed his foot on the first step and looked over. "I don't suppose you have room service? I have had nothing to eat in quite a while."

"No, we don't. But I think we have some leftovers from dinner. I will send someone up with them."

"Thank you again." Sanford continued up the steps, opened the old wooden door with a scratched metal "2" on it and went inside. The Lilliputian-sized simple room only had a full size spring mattress and a dresser with three drawers. A phone the likes of which hadn't been sold in twenty-five years sat on the dresser. The room did have an attached bathroom, its one positive feature.

There wasn't any dust, but he decided not to look under the bed. He had a hunch he wouldn't want to sleep there if he did. He dragged the dresser over to the bed and sat the processing core on it. The bag of power cells he dropped by his feet as he sat on the bed.

He needed equipment, or at least a small monitor, keyboard, and mouse. His eyes gleamed when he remembered a used computer store he passed on his way here. Sanford stood up, walked out of the room, locked the door, and headed down the steps. The woman had retreated into the backroom and didn't see him leave.

Sanford walked quickly down the street. He saw several people on the sidewalk, but they paid no attention to him. Several blocks away he found the used computer store. He went around the back and flipped up the top on a large dumpster. Thankful the store didn't share it with a fast-food restaurant, he started digging around. After several minutes he found what he was after: an older model keyboard, a dirty mouse, and a flat screen with a smashed area where the power switch should be.

He tucked all three items into the bag he brought and

headed back to the inn. The door jingled, and the woman came out again. "I wondered where you went. I sent my son up with some leftovers and you didn't answer the door. I assumed there was a problem, so I opened the door and found you gone."

Sanford smiled again. "Sorry, I needed to get a few things." He patted the bag at his hip.

The woman's eyebrow raised as her hands went to her hips. "And how did you afford this?"

"It was all stuff from their dumpster. I didn't think they would mind."

The woman's stern look softened. "Oh, I see. If you are still hungry, I will send up those leftovers."

"Yes. Thank you." Sanford said, heading up the steps to his room. Each step creaked louder than the last.

He slipped the key in the lock, opened the door and went inside. He sat on the bed and pulled out the dirty keyboard, broken monitor, and grimy mouse. Popping off the front cover of monitor he found while the switch was gone, the wires were still intact. He twisted the two leads together, plugged it into the processing core, followed by the mouse, keyboard, and powered up the core.

The screen remained inky black. Sanford held his breath. *Had the core been damaged on my way here?* Several more seconds passed before the screen jumped to life displaying the usual boot up sequence. Sanford wiped his forehead. The salvaged equipment was far below his standards and caused the core to reconfigure, but it was *working*. He heard a soft knock at the door and stood up. "It's open."

The door opened a crack and a boy about eight years old wearing jeans and a worn baseball jersey peeked around. "Hi, my Mom said to bring this up?" He swung a covered plate around the door and into the room.

Sanford walked over and took the plate. "Great. Thanks."

"Sure." The head disappeared back around the door and it clicked shut. Sanford walked over and locked it to make sure the boy wouldn't peek in again. His Mother could, but he would deal with her if and when the time came.

Lifting the cover on the plate, he saw two pieces of bread and some bits of chicken. It wasn't the most appetizing, but in truth it was the best-looking thing he had seen at the inn. He sat on the bed devouring the food, not realizing how hungry he was until the first piece touched his lips.

He turned his attention back to the core and plugged in a network cable and the other end into an old wall jack he found hidden behind the dresser. The old connection and questionable cable he recovered from the dumpster would make his connection a great deal slower than what he was used to, but it would be enough. Once online, first thing Sanford did was transfer money to his old account at the local bank. Then he ordered a few more items he would need.

Red stirred and her eyes fluttered open as she sat up. Her head spun, and she leaned back against the couch for a few minutes. "Ugh, I hate when I do that!"

No response.

"Anyone around?" Red called, but the only sound was the air conditioning cycling on. She went from room to room, not finding James, Keleeigan, or even Trisia. Red scratched her head. "This doesn't make sense. They wouldn't leave me."

Her eyes flashed. "Unless Sanford did something, and they had no choice."

She looked out where Keleeigan kept his car, but she didn't see it. She went down into the basement and found one of the screens still on. She blinked when she saw James talking, although she couldn't quite make out the words as his face was turned away from the apparent camera. He moved and Trisia stood next to him. When she moved to the other side, she could see Keleeigan hunched over a workstation.

She didn't know how to turn the camera, if it could be turned, but she thought she recognized the one wall. She tapped her earpiece. "Hey, do you hear me? Or are we out of range?"

She saw James jump, then tap his ear. "Red! You're awake! I'm sorry, I didn't think you would be for several hours yet."

"Where are you?"

"In Keleeigan's main lab."

"I know that, I see you. I should have said why are you there?"

James blinked and looked around. "You can see us?"

"I'm Keleeigan's basement. He left the screen on and I see you on it. I'm guessing Sanford was up to something?"

"You could say that. Sanford was here."

"What? I thought you had gone there because Keleeigan needed something."

"I wish that were true. Sanford did eventually trip an alarm, but Doc didn't find out for a while because he warped in bypassing most of the alarms and security."

"Figures. What was he doing there? I assume he didn't get anything if I know Keleeigan."

"You know Doc yes, but Sanford did get away with some information."

Red's face scrunched up. This didn't sound good. "What kind of information?"

"Well … how about the possible ability to create temporal warps?"

"WHAT! How? Didn't Keleeigan have everything locked down?"

James sighed. "He did, but Sanford used a data recovery program and managed to find a partial file which wasn't completely wiped when trashed as it should have been. It wasn't the whole formula Doc used for his temporal field, but it might be enough given what Sanford already knows. However, it was an older version, so Doc isn't 100% sure he could get it to work."

"Did you find out where he went?"

James shook his head on the screen. "No. By the time we got there, he was long gone and Atrus couldn't track him."

"Great. A mad man with a possible method to travel into the past and wreck untold damage to the time-line. Even worse, we have no idea where he went or how to find out."

"We did come up with an idea that might work."

Trisia touched her ear. "Yes, we did. Although it started with me."

"Fine, you did. Anyway, we figure Sanford will have to make a phone call sooner or later. When he does, we will know where he is."

"And how do you plan to do that?" Red said.

"Atrus of course."

"Atrus can't scan the whole world's communication system 24/7."

"No, he can't. There will be gaps. But Trisia thinks he will stick to the United States, and that lowers the search by a large margin."

"That is still one heck of a lot of calls to monitor day and night."

Atrus looked up into the camera. "But they have determined Sanford prefers day to night, and I am centering my efforts during those hours."

Red folded her arms. "Makes sense. Now are you going to come and get me? Or do I have to warp there myself?"

James laughed. "I will get you."

Keleeigan looked up and Red saw his mouth move but couldn't quite catch the words. "Doc says we will back soon. He is reconfiguring the security here so Sanford won't be able to set foot inside without every alarm in the place going off," James said.

"Okay see you soon." Red said sat down in a padded chair next to one of the lab tables and leaned back. Nothing to do but wait and try to recover her energy. She was sure they were going to need every bit she had.

A few hours later, Keleeigan's car landed outside the house. Red stood by the front door and James ran up to her, grabbed her, and kissed her soft lips. "I'm so glad you are okay."

Her eyebrows met. "If you were so worried, why did you leave me?"

"I ... that is ... it was ... "

Red's face softened. "Sanford arrived, and you knew I couldn't help for a while so you went on alone. I know. But next time, leave a note, will you?"

James pointed to his ear. "You could have called. Atrus says they will work anywhere in the world."

Red cocked her head. "Since when?"

"Since he reprogrammed them to access the current phone system if we are out of the usual range."

"But won't someone be able to hear us? I don't want to be overheard when we are talking about temporal warps or such."

Atrus flashed on to Red's right. "That is not possible. All communications between the A.T.E. and myself are encrypted with a method which is unbreakable in this time. In fact, it was unbreakable in mine as well."

Red rolled her eyes. "He likes to do that a bit too much."

Trisia walked up. "Likes to do what?"

She glared at Atrus. "Show off!"

Atrus smiled and disappeared.

Sanford smiled as he keyed in several commands. His room had changed in the last few weeks. A small desk and chair sat wedged in the corner. It blocked the bathroom door to a large degree, but it fit. And special deliveries continued to arrive on a regular basis. The inn owner wondered, but being he paid every day, sometimes several in advance, she didn't say a word and left him alone.

Her son was another matter. Several times he noticed the boy trying to peek inside his room or even slip inside. He didn't like how the boy had gathered such an interest in him, but since he didn't know anything, Sanford didn't take any action.

He went to his window, pulled it open, and checked the pole he had attached to the side of the building. It wasn't a proper lightning rod, and he doubted it would hold up for more than one attempt, but one attempt is all he needed. Or at least hoped. He had expected the son or owner to ask him about it, but being he was on the side facing a row of trees, they didn't notice. All was ready. And had been for some time.

Sanford paced back and forth in his room. The floor creaking with each step. "So close, so very close. I can almost taste it. I will get my revenge against them all. Not one will ever have been born!" He paced some more and consulted several weather watching sites. Three of them predicted a large storm approaching, but no details. And he needed details.

He grumbled and decided there wasn't any choice. He picked up the phone in his room and entered the number for the local NOAA office. "Yes?" A female voice answered. "Can we help you?"

"I hope so. I have a bet going with a friend, and I was wondering if the approaching storm has any potential for lightning? I have checked your site, but it doesn't list a live radar feed."

"Yes, I'm sorry. We are in the process of upgrading it. But to answer your question, yes it does."

"Can you be more specific?"

"It is on a southwest trajectory and should arrive in twenty minutes. We are expecting hail in the storm as well."

Sanford leaned out the window, seeing the dark clouds again rolling towards him. "Oh, thank you. I have won the bet."

"You and your buddy aren't going out in it, are you?"

"Certainly not. I'm not a crazy person."

"Good. Have a nice day." The phone clicked off.

Sanford shut the window and started rubbing his hands

together. Twenty minutes now seemed like weeks. But he knew today would be the day.

17

Red paced back and forth in Keleeigan's cramped basement. "Weeks without so much as a trace of Sanford."

James watched her move back and forth. "Perhaps he couldn't figure it out?"

Red stopped, turned her head, and glared at him. "Do you honestly think he couldn't?"

James shrugged. "Doc even said it was possible."

Keleeigan's head popped up from behind his monitor. "I said it was possible yes, not probable."

"Meaning it is a large bet he could do it. I know, I know. But it seems odd he hasn't done anything yet," James said.

"You're telling me. I'm starting to think Atrus missed him," Red said.

Atrus flashed on in front of her. "I do not think I have. The monitoring has been consistent with the time frame indicated as the most probable."

Red glared. "Atrus your hologram? You need all the power you can find to monitor and track."

Atrus sighed. "I know, but I still like to appear on occasion." His image flickered and vanished.

James stood up from the sofa where he was sitting with Trisia and walked over to Keleeigan. "Doc? I would have thought your time travel system would be operational by now."

"It is, or at least should be. I still need to run a few tests. And I need to install it back inside the lighthouse or something else before it is useable."

James' eyebrow raised as he cocked his head. "The lighthouse? I thought it was done for?"

"Not quite. It needs work, yes, but it is not a total loss. Not to mention with my equipment working at 100% it should be a smooth trip."

Red paced faster. "I don't think taking that building through time is a good idea. We got lucky before, but what happens if someone from the past sees it and alters the future as a result."

James shrugged. "It is a lighthouse, I mean a plain building, what could change someone by a profound measure? Now, if they saw it land, that could do it."

Red spun around. "That's what I am talking about! It is too big. When I generate warps we sneak in between buildings, behind trees or some other location that is hidden. It is harder to impossible to hide a big building when it arrives out of nowhere."

Keleeigan coughed. "Indeed, but I can't do time jumps like you can. It takes a lot of equipment and a building to house it."

"Doc, wouldn't it be better to use something more mobile?" James said.

"With the energy requirements we are talking about? No. I also need good grounding when I generate the temporal field. It won't work otherwise."

"Why not use some sort of big bus? For grounding, you could rig a rod to extend into the dirt."

Keleeigan cocked his head. "A rod to stick into the ground? You mean go outside and hammer that in every time? No thanks."

"Nah, most buses or motor homes have hydraulic levelers that extend out at the touch of a button. Why couldn't you rig one to drive a rod into the ground?"

Keleeigan eyes flashed. "That might work!"

"But without roads, moving it around could be problematic. So it could negate any positives," Trisia said.

Keleeigan rubbed his chin. "Oh, but I may have a solution to that little problem."

"Oh? Which is?"

"It is quite simple, I–"

Atrus flashed on in front of them. He faced each of them in turn. "I am sorry to interrupt, but I have found Sanford."

"Where?" Red said.

"Maine. To be more specific, the city known as Eastport."

"Anything more than that?" James said.

"Unfortunately yes, the communication was with the NOAA agency about the probability of lightning storms in the area. I suspect he has created some sort of device to harness the last component he needs for a temporal warp," Atrus said.

"Do you have the exact coordinates?" Red said.

Atrus nodded. "Affirmative. He is at a small inn on the very edge of the city limits. Room '2' to be exact. I have accessed the owner's system, and she has only one tenant at the moment."

Red headed for the steps. "Let's go stop him."

"Would it be better to go there with Doc's car?" James said.

"It will take too long. He might be gone by then."

"Might, that is a big might."

"Listen, you should know better than anyone else the dangers if the time-line is messed with or damaged. While I too doubt Sanford can pull it off this soon with what he has, it is not worth the risk," Red said.

James raised his hands. "Okay, I was just pointing out that if you are too tired and we need to jump to follow him. Then what? This will drain you, and we will need you more to follow him. We can drive there. Or rather fly."

"It will still take hours, it is a short jump for me. And I will still be able to open a temporal warp if we need. Now, come on, we're wasting time."

James sighed as he grabbed the backpack and followed her with Trisia right behind. "We're coming, we're coming."

Keleeigan turned, his old desk chair squeaking as he did. "I will watch from here. With my new equipment, I should be able to track him should he succeed in a temporal jump."

James stood at the door at the top of the basement and turned around. "Doc? I thought you said it all had to be installed back at the lighthouse?"

"I said a building. While I can't temporal jump with this house, as it is far too big, my equipment still works here. And I can track any sort of temporal shifts. If he does a temporal wiggle, I will see it."

James nodded as he continued up the steps. "Right. See you soon, Doc."

He found Red and Trisia in Doc's backyard. Red bent over, stretching. "Ready?"

James and Trisia both nodded. "Ready."

Red lowered herself into a sprinting position and shot like a bolt gaining speed around them. The air began to swirl causing a cloud of dust to form behind Red. She pushed a little harder and the clouds rolled in. A second later several forks of energy reached out from the clouds, combined, and streaked for the ground. When they touched, a vast arc of power lit up the area. In its wake a red crack in the very fabric of space and time glowed. The crack flickered, retracted, then shot out, growing into a red oval ripple that fluctuated between red and black. The colors continued to shift as red shouted. "Go! What are you waiting for?"

"For you to say it!" James shouted as he and Trisia ran for the warp. Trisia made it there first, being a couple of steps closer, followed by James, and a second later by Red. The warp grew larger then slammed shut, leaving a glowing line for several seconds before fading.

The rain pelted the window as Sanford looked up from the old monitor. If all went well, tonight he would be on his way. He sat back in his desk chair, rotating it left and right. He wasn't nervous by any means, but this was a great unknown. Even if he could open a stable aperture, it wouldn't last long. While his dimensional doors would stay open for as long as he wanted, or at least had power for. This was much more problematic. He ran his calculations again. Nothing had changed since the last few hundred times he had run them, but he wanted to be certain. There would be no margin for error.

Or if there was, it could only be slight. But then he would miss his target by a great deal. He could even end up in the middle of the ocean, the more benign of several very bad possible outcomes.

He checked the sensors he had placed on the roof.

Putting them there without the owner knowing was another interesting challenge, but he accomplished it. The ions in the air looked favorable, and they were increasing. He tapped several more keys and bought up a map; it wasn't real-time but it did show where the storm was over ten minutes ago and its course. Sanford did several calculations in his head and knew the center of the storm would be here in two minutes, if not sooner.

The air rippled and swirled around a point between two large trees. Lighting struck the center, and a crack formed in its wake. The crack mushroomed into an area large enough for a man to pass through.

Trisia landed with a thud on the wet grass. She looked up through the rain hitting her face to see James emerging. She rolled to the side as he landed face down and almost kissed the dirt. He saw where Trisia was and rolled to the other side, rubbing his hip where he hit. Red emerged and landed on her feet in a crouching position. The warp flickered, condensed down to a point, and disappeared.

Red stood up. The rain ran down her face as she looked up. "Well, we must be in the right place, or very close to it."

"Do you doubt my coordinates?" Atrus said.

"No. Where is the inn from here? And no hologram?"

"It is to your right, down the road, then take a left at the first available turn. And my energy is running low, I must conserve it." Atrus said.

Red nodded as James and Trisia stood up. "Let's move," James said, "if nothing else to get out of this rain. I'm getting soaked."

"Me too," Trisia shivered. It wasn't a cold night, but the rain and wind were having a cooling effect. "I'm freezing too."

"It isn't that bad," James said.

"Speak for yourself."

They headed for the Inn as a lightning bolt flashed down from the heavens and struck something not far away.

Sanford looked out at the several flashes of light in the sky. They were getting closer by the second. He flipped the spring-loaded latch on the old double-hung window and opened it again. Rain started blowing in along with several leaves from the trees on the other side of the window. The aging wooden floor had already seen more moisture than it had in years, but this was only the start.

Sanford connected a spring-loaded claw to the pole he had attached by his window. He hit a button on the side and the pole extended itself many feet into the air. Another flash and a loud crack of thunder as a large surge of power hit the ground not far away. The claw ended in a large cable attached to a round cylindrical device. He wasn't sure how much this capacitor could hold, but he hoped it was enough. The Keleeigan's formula said the energy had to be placed all at once or it wouldn't work. Timing was everything.

He tapped a few keys and slung a large bag over his shoulder. It had to be soon. It had to be.

He didn't have time to turn his head before a large flash blinded his peripheral vision. A large concentrated lightning bolt hit his pole, followed down the line, and crashed into the capacitor. Smoke filled the room, and the capacitor glowed white-hot. Sanford connected a cable to the device on his chest. Energy flashed into it from the capacitor. He held his breath as power continued to flow, but no warp appeared. Five seconds later–which felt like an eternity to Sanford–an arc of energy erupted from his chest, reaching out and hitting the wall where Sanford was looking. The energy went up and down, tracing an invisible line. In its wake left a large red, glowing crack.

Sanford watched as the crack open as if someone unzipped their pants. It folded open, revealing a flashing red and black warp. Sanford smiled. He had done it! A temporal warp created using the Keleeigan's formula stood before him. The flashing chaotic mass of energy rippled and swayed as much as the trees outside. Yet not moving from its position in the room.

"Sanford! Stop! You don't know what you are doing!" A voice called from the other side of the wooden door.

Sanford knew the voice. It was the voice of the lady with red hair. The one Trisia had spoke of and met in his first lab. They had found him! "I know exactly what I'm doing! Getting my revenge! Against you, against everyone!"

James began ramming his shoulder against the door. "Dang it, these old doors are a lot stronger."

"Get out of the way." Red said as she placed her hand on the lock. The lock panel vibrated, and the door swung open.

They ran in, just in time to see Sanford disappear into the warp. James ran for it but it slammed shut a microsecond before he reached the red-black vortex. The capacitor burst into flames. A power surge ran from it over to the computational core causing it, the monitor, keyboard, and mouse to spark and burn. The room filled with the smell of burnt electronics, plastic, and wood.

"I'll get something to put this out." James said as he ran

downstairs. He returned three seconds later with a large red metal cylinder. He sprayed the room with its chemical foam and the fire was out a few moments later.

Trisia looked at James. "Why didn't you blast the door with that fancy gun you have?"

"I didn't want to take the chance of someone seeing," he whispered.

"I wish you did," Red said, "he got away."

"You could have popped the lock on the door two steps before I got here. Why didn't you do that? Hmm?"

"I wanted to warn him. Give him one last chance."

"One last chance to do what? Kill us all? Weren't you the one that was warning us with all the damage he could do?"

Red spat. "I was. But I hoped he might listen to me. And I thought we could get through the door before he could jump. If we ran in earlier, he would have jumped a few seconds sooner. It wouldn't have made any difference."

James sighed. "You're right."

A woman appeared behind them. "What in the world is going on here? Is something on fire?" She stepped into the room and sucked in a breath. "My room! What have you done to it?"

Red put on her best smile. "We didn't, the guy in here did."

The woman blinked. "Linus? He wouldn't have done this. Heck, he paid me extra and a month in advance once he got access to his money."

Trisia turned. "His money? What happened?"

The woman shrugged. "He didn't go into details. He lost his wallet and I got the feeling something else happened. He didn't have a thing with him except a bag over his shoulder, and that," she paused to point at the large plastic, now very melted rectangle sitting on the desk Sanford had bought, "under his arm."

"Did he say anything when he was here?"

"Not much. Quietest tenant I ever had. Nicest too, he told me I could keep the furniture he bought. But I don't think I would have let him bring this stuff in otherwise." She looked around the room again, waving her arms. "Now look at it! I will have to hire someone to fix the place up." Rain started again through the window and she ran to slam it shut. "And what was this open for? Its made a mess of the floor!"

Red shrugged. "Again, we didn't do it. We just got here. As you can see Sanford opened the door for us, then he ran out."

"Sanford? Is that Linus' last name? He never did tell me. And you say he ran out? I didn't see anyone leave. Just you three come in."

James had enough of this. He pulled out his wallet, flipped it open. His FBI badge hung a few inches from the woman's face. "I am Agent Moknkin. The man you know as Linus is a person of interest we need to find. If he comes back alert me at once." James flipped his wallet closed and handed her a card with his number on it.

The woman blinked several times before taking the card. "FBI? Is he in that much trouble? Am I in trouble for helping him?"

James shook his head. "No, you didn't know. But I do request you tell no one of this incident."

The woman nodded. "Certainly. Do you need me to preserve the room?"

"No, feel free to have it repaired. If you need assistance, call the number and I will provide it. But you told us he paid extra."

The woman nodded again. "Yes, he did. Quite a bit. I will be able to fix the room with ease, and a few other parts of the inn I have wanted to have repaired."

"Then we will leave you too it. Nice meeting you." James pointed to the door and left with Trisia and Red right after.

They left by the front door and the storm had subsided by now, even though they were all soaked. "Atrus? Did you find where Sanford went to?"

"Yes. Ancient Mesopotamia. To be more specific, the city of Babylon May 20th 582 BC."

"What? We have to follow him!"

James wiped away a drop which threatened to run into his left eye. "Can we? Are you rested enough to open a warp that far into the past?"

"I have to be. Babylon was a center point of humanity then. If he sets off one of those modified power cells there, the damage would ripple through the time-line like a tsunami destroying all we know. Humanity might survive, but it would alter everything so much I can't even imagine how vast the changes would be."

They found a small vacant lot, but the ground was too slippery for Red to get a footing at high speed. They moved on down the sidewalks, trying to find a location large enough and yet not very prominent. They struck pay dirt, finding a small parking lot behind a dentist. Trisia looked around. "I don't see anyone."

Red stretched and ran in place for a few seconds trying to warm up. The rain had chilled her. While her bodysuit had almost dried thanks to its special fabric, she was still cold. "Yes. I hope it is large enough. I would prefer a bit more room."

James smiled. "You did mange it in one of our integration rooms if you remember."

Red chuckled. "How could I forget?"

Trisia blinked. "Wait, what?"

"It is where I met Red, in one of the integration rooms at the FBI. Although, met is not quite the right word. I was sucked into one of her warps there."

Trisia blinked again. "Sometime I want to hear this story, it sounds like a good one."

"It is, trust me."

Atrus beeped. "I am sorry to interrupt, but I am detecting a massive temporal disturbance heading this way."

"Dang it! How long until it gets here?"

"Hard to estimate, perhaps one minute," Atrus said.

Red lowered herself into position. "I hope I can punch through it." Red shot off, running faster and faster. The air began to swirl.

Atrus beeped again. "Thirty seconds."

"Red?" James said with a slight quiver in his voice.

"I know ... it ... is ... being ... difficult."

"What's going on?" Trisia shouted.

"If I understand it right, Sanford changed something in the past and the temporal changes are heading for us. If it catches us like this, we may cease to exist. But because of the temporal fluctuations Red is having trouble creating a warp."

"James! The headband!"

"Right!" James whipped open his bag, pulled out a headband with a crystalline section mounted on the elastic, and threw it towards Red. She jumped, grabbed it, slipped it on her forehead, and kept on running.

Trisia blinked. "Headband?"

"It's a special crystal which boosts her accuracy and range. And right now we need all we can get for her to punch through the interference."

Atrus beeped again. "Twenty seconds."

"Red? We really need a warp about now."

"Shut … it … am … trying."

Lightning struck the center of the parking lot, and a crack appeared. The center of it sparked, flashed, grew, then receded.

"That's it! You almost have it!"

Red pushed and the crack spread, but slower than James had ever seen before.

"Ten seconds," Atrus said, "and keep in mind these are only estimates."

"Red!"

"I … can't … sorry …"

"I'm sorry too." James pulled out his gun, keyed in a sonic setting he knew well and fired it near Red's wake.

"Noooooo! James! You promised! *Noooo!*" Red's speed increased several times and their ears rang from the sonic boom. The warp quickly mushroomed from a small crack to something large enough for a truck to drive through.

"Five seconds," Atrus said.

James grabbed Trisia's arm. "We have to go now!" He ran and pulled her into the warp with him. Red followed a microsecond later.

As they entered, Atrus hoped the transmission penetrated the temporal interference.

The warp slammed shut with a thunderous crack, blowing out all the windows in every building for miles a second before a strange energy wave washed over everything. For a moment everything stood unchanged, then the buildings began to grow translucent, growing fainter by the second. When it had passed, nothing remained except grass and a large forest where a city once stood.

18

A spark flashed along the center of a mud-brick wall. Then another, arching together to form a jagged rip. It flickered, then expanded vertically. A few seconds later it expanded horizontally but stopped short of its normal size. The warp flickered, flashed between black and red. Sanford dove through the portal. His arm hit the packed dirt first, and he tried to roll. Instead of spreading out his momentum as planned, his face hit the dirt along with the rest of him a second later. The temporal warp slammed shut with a loud crack. Vile smells assaulted his nostrils as he spit several kinds of crud and felt his left arm. It hurt, but nothing broken. He stood up–thankful he hadn't landed in one of the many garbage heaps all over the street–and walked to the other side of the building three seconds before two people walked by looking up at the clear sky.

Looking for the signs of rain no doubt, when the portal closed it did sound like thunder. He checked the charge on his cloak and swore. *It took all I had getting here.* Sanford looked across the crooked street and saw a small two-story house on the opposite side. It was early morning and still cool. Sanford approached the house and entered through the open door. No sign of its occupants, but he did find a smaller room along the back wall. He entered and sat in the corner. He pulled out a power cell out of his bag and a couple of tools he had brought. In a few minutes he had the top off, and pulling out one of the internal connecters. He carefully plugged the connector into a small port on his belt and waited.

After a few moments, the cell glowed as it transferred power to the cloak. Sanford thought he heard something but when he looked up, no one was there. Three minutes later the light on his belt showed a full charge. He unplugged the power cell and checked it. He had used a third of its internal charge, but it would recover in an hour or two.

He reassembled the power cell, put it back in his bag along with the tools, and stood up. Looking around to make sure no one was watching, he pressed a button on his belt and vanished. A slight impression remained in the dirt floor where he sat and scuffed it out with his foot. *No sense leaving any calling cards if I can avoid it.* He left the house, smiled as his eyes drifted up to the large structure dominating the skyline, and headed towards it.

Lightning struck, and a zigzag rip appeared in its wake. The crack flickered and flashed until it grew many times its size, revealing a spinning mass of concentrated energy. Trisia fell out of the warp and rolled to the side a second before James came through, landed on his feet and spun around in time to catch Red. The warp slammed shut with a thunderous crack.

James' head flipped back and forth. They were in an ancient city judging by the high walls and various decaying matter in the streets. At least they didn't land on any. Several pigs ran passed, stopping nearby to feast on disposed flesh. "Atrus, someone was bound to hear that. A little camouflage, please."

"My resources are running low but I will have enough for a brief period."

"Do it. I think I hear people coming."

"Yes, someone is approaching. Stand as close together as possible."

Trisia stood up and moved closer as Red stirred. "Did ... we ... make it?"

"Yes, now rest."

"Okay ..." Red's breathing came in slow rhythmic as Atrus activated a hologram making the mud-brick wall appear a little further out into the disgusting street.

A man appeared in a long wool tunic. Looking around the corner. He spoke something neither of them could understand and moved on.

The holographic wall vanished. "I have enough resources for two more minutes," Atrus said.

"We need to find a place to hide out until Red recovers."

"Don't look at me, I have no idea. And at the moment I wish I stayed home," Trisia said.

"And be erased from existence?"

"No, you have a point. And what did you do with Red? I didn't think she had enough energy. She also shouted something about you promised?"

"By accident I discovered a certain sonic blast strengthens Red and enables her to do more than she is normally able to. But it takes her longer to recover."

"So she is out for the count."

James nodded. "Yes, for a while anyway. Let's find someplace to hide out."

The smell of rotting fruit and flesh caused Trisia's nose to wrinkle. "And somewhere that doesn't smell so bad." She waved a hand in front of her nose. "Geez, haven't these people ever heard of trash disposal?"

"Actually, the streets are their trash disposal. If you mean sewers or otherwise carrying it away and out of the city, the concept won't be commonplace for hundreds of years," Atrus said.

Trisia rolled her eyes. "Great. Just what I always wanted to do, go traipsing through a dirty, disgusting city."

"It should be more pleasant inside the buildings. However, the odors might still be prevalent. It is possible this is why perfume was developed in the first place."

James looked around. "Atrus, while I like your information, could you find a place we can go? I'm carrying Red, remember?"

"Certainly. Take the road to the right, turn left, then right, then left again and you will find a small empty house with a storage area in back."

Trisia blinked. "And you know this how?"

"I have a map of this period Babylon. I can show you if you prefer."

"No, save your energy. And right, left, then left again?" James said.

"I will direct you," Atrus said.

They walked through the tangle of streets and reached the house Atrus spoke of. It was a modest two story building near the city wall, but was empty except for what was a part of the house itself.

"I don't get it. Why would this house be empty? It is still in good shape. Or is someone trying to sell it?" Trisia said.

James lay Red down on the worn mud brick floor in a

room around the corner from the entrance and closed the front door. He sat down next to her, slipped headband from her forehead, and stuffed it back into his bag. "If anyone comes, we should have enough warning to move to the back rooms Atrus mentioned. As for why no one is here, perhaps someone died and they haven't found a new owner yet."

"Maybe." Trisia left and returned a few minutes later. "This place is a like their streets, a winding labyrinth. Didn't Babylonians ever hear of simple floor plans?"

"At the moment, it is to our advantage. I hope Sanford doesn't do anything while we wait." James pulled out Atrus and pushed the button on the flat bottom of the cylindrical device. They heard a slight beep as the recharging system engaged. "And now we are blind for a while."

"And hungry. We haven't eaten anything since Keleeigan's. And how long ago was that?"

James smiled. "Kind of hard to tell in this business." He reached in his bag and flipped a small wrapped bar towards Trisia. She caught it in midair. "Nice catch. It's an energy bar. It may not be filet mignon, but it will fill your stomach and keep your energy up."

Trisia pealed off the wrapper and held it up. "Here. I am sure you don't want to leave this around for someone to find."

"There is a little tab on the right. Pull it, then touch the center of the part that extends out."

Trisia found the small plastic tab, pulled it which revealed a little black circular area on the now extended part of the plastic and touched it. The wrapper grew warm in her hands, then disappeared. "Whoa! What happened?"

"Like it, eh? We get these from the future. As you can see, they don't have any trouble with landfills."

Trisia took a bite and chewed. "Not bad. A little plain, but not bad."

"There are better tasting ones, but they don't last as long in your stomach. We always wanted them to last as long as possible for obvious reasons."

Trisia took another bite. "I can understand that. Sure tastes better than some things I was eating a year ago." She paused thinking, then laughed.

James cocked his head. "What are you laughing for?"

Trisia tried to stop, then laughed all the harder. "I'm sorry, but it just hit me a year ago is many centuries from now."

James smiled. "I have to admit, I never bothered thinking about it and I have been traveling with Red for quite a while. Although we are usually running from something or someone."

"Might take your mind off of what you were doing," Trisia said as she took the last bite and swallowed.

"Yes, it did. And then some." James looked at the thick wall which gave way to the next room. "Another advantage of Babylonian architecture, with these thick walls, no one should hear us in here."

Trisia looked over. "So what do we do now?"

"We wait and hope Sanford doesn't do anything while we are."

Sanford continued walking along the maze the Babylonians called streets. Several times he almost lost the contents of his stomach as he passed over decaying animal and plant remains, among other forms of garbage. He couldn't understand how people could live like this. The various buildings were at least decent inside. But the smell followed you everywhere. Several times he had to step to the side or risk running someone over. Or have them run into him. Being invisible, it wouldn't do to have someone fall backwards for no apparent reason. It might induce a mass panic in this primitive society.

He thought about revealing himself, and they would assume him to be a god and submit themselves to him. But too many things could go wrong. It would threaten their current beliefs system, and those in charge of the current system would not be pleased. He might find himself murdered in his sleep, or have someone try to prove he is a man not a god by his death before he could complete his task.

The idea made him shudder. No, it was better to maintain a low profile, and finish what he had come for. Sanford turned again, continuing towards the ziggurat on the horizon.

He stopped and stared for several meters ahead of him stood a woman with long red hair. Clothed in a Babylonian tunic, it reached below her knees with fringe on each side. He blinked. *It is the woman I just escaped from. How could she be here before me?*

Sanford's mind raced, and an invisible palm hit an invisible forehead with a slight slap. *She could if she tracked when I arrived and set her destination before me.* He looked around but didn't see Trisia or the man he saw with them before. They had to be somewhere.

The woman continued walking, and Sanford followed. He waited until she turned down an otherwise empty street before firing a pellet into her neck. She stopped mid-step; he grabbed her, and extended his cloak. She vanished from sight before anyone could notice.

A few hours later Red awoke in a small mud brick room with a single window blocked by terra cotta mesh. While still early afternoon, the small window only let in enough light to see rough outlines to keep from tripping over anything. She blinked several times, trying to see more within the dim room. She couldn't remember what happened. Last she knew she was walking down the street when … something happened. Next thing she knew, she was here. The smell wafting in from the window told her she was still in Babylon, but how could anyone have taken her without her knowledge?

Her hands were bound behind her back, and she tried to sit up from the mud brick floor. After several tries, she made it. The door opened and closed, but no one entered. The strangest thing, she didn't see anyone open it, let alone close it. Red cocked her head. "Hello?"

"Ah, you can speak. So glad my concoction wasn't too much for you. I had to adjust it on-the-fly as it were due to your interference and I wasn't sure of the full outcome."

Red blinked again. The voice spoke English. How could this be? "I hear you, but I don't see you. Are you standing outside the door?"

"Not at all. I am right next to you." Sanford touched Red's cheek and she recoiled. "And I know you felt that."

"Who or what are you?"

Sanford laughed. "Oh the dumb routine, I love it. Please, try harder. Although, I'm enjoying this immensely."

"I don't know who you are, or what you want."

"Oh you do. I can't imagine how you could forget since you have been chasing me all over, foiling every plan I have made. If you would have just let me be. Although, I suppose if someone had tried to kill me I wouldn't be very inclined to leave them alone either."

Red blinked again. "I don't understand."

Sanford felt for his belt and pushed a button on it. The edges of his form began to reflect light again, growing until a man-shaped blob stood in front of Red. The blob grew less transparent as it revealed a smiling man beneath.

Red blinked yet again and cocked her head. "Who are you? I don't recognize you or your technology."

Sanford looked into her eyes. "You don't know me, do you? How is this possible?"

"You tell me, you seem to have all the answers," Red said.

"This makes little sense unless … this is a previous version of you and you haven't met me yet."

Red blinked again. This man not only seemed to know her, but also had temporal travel as well. "Previous version of me? Not sure I understand you."

Sanford glared. "Please don't insult my intelligence with such statements. I know you travel through time, and from you I found a way to wedge open a temporal warp."

"Not possible."

"It is. But if it is any consolation, I had to pry it from you. Or rather your digital assistant."

"My what?"

"Oh, sorry you don't know about that yet either, do you? Oh this could be so much fun, but I regret it has complicated my plans. While I could kill you, it might affect what I'm doing now. If I leave you here, while no one will look inside this storage room for several days, I can't take the risk you might die. Hmm, you have left me with a rather large problem."

Red smiled. "You could let me go."

"I could, but then I don't know what you might do. You can see my dilemma, I'm sure."

"What if I promise to leave here as soon as I can?"

"Wish I could believe you, but sorry I don't." Sanford took several steps towards the door. "I guess I will have to take the risk and leave you here for now. Enjoy the accommodations." He opened the door and stepped through.

"Wait! You said yourself you can't let me die or it will disrupt your own time-line. I have to assume you are planning something I would normally want to stop, which has to be a large intrusion into the time-line. And if so, and if you go through with it, wouldn't I die anyway?"

Sanford reached for the door and closed it half-way. "Very true, but at that point I won't care." He slammed the door shut, and she heard something brace the door from the outside.

Red sat in the dim room trying to remove the tight cloth, keeping her hands tied behind her back. The man was insane. He had to be planning something horrible. And the only thing that made sense was the city itself. But if he created an event, and she was at ground zero as was he, it wouldn't matter if he killed her now or later. Being he found out how to move through time from her and further on in her time-line, it would create a massive paradox. The paradox on that scale would rip throughout the time-line like a tsunami destroying everything. The repercussions were beyond imagination. No one had done it, and she didn't want to be the center of the largest paradox ever. And even if she survived, because she was at the center of it, Red doubted she could repair the damage. And she was the only one that could.

Red ran her hands back and forth faster and faster inside the cloth. It started to heat, then her speed reduced. She tried again, but her arms refused to obey. She bit her lip realizing she hadn't recovered from the previous jump yet. She was trapped. And worse, she was the part of the reason even if from the future.

19

Red stirred as she sat up and rubbed her pounding head. "Ow! Who dropped an anvil on my head?"

James ran over and wrapped his arms around her in a tight squeeze. "I'm sorry but I knew you couldn't do it without my help."

Red reached around his arm and rubbed her forehead again. "I might forgive you, but not today," James sighed releasing her, "how long have I been out?"

"About eight hours," Trisia said.

Red's eyes drifted, down focusing on what they were wearing. "I take it no one has tried to find clothes for us?"

"No, I didn't think it was wise wandering around in a suit. It would attract way too much attention."

Red blinked. "What about Atrus?"

Trisia sighed. "His battery ran out."

"Yes, and he is still recharging. He should be done soon," James said.

"Why didn't you try when he had recovered enough of a charge?"

"I thought it was better to wait. After all, who knows, we might need Atrus' abilities more later."

"Maybe, but we need to–." Red tried to stand, then

stumbled, and James helped her back down to the mud brick floor.

"Easy, you are not back yet."

"I have to be. We have to find Sanford. He has arrived by now."

Trisia blinked. "What do you mean arrived by now? He was here when we landed."

Red shook her head and wished she hadn't. "No, he wasn't. You see, I altered our exit point a little, so we would arrive before him. But I only factored in a few hours lead time. We missed our chance to grab him as soon as he arrived."

"It isn't your fault," James said.

"No, it is yours," Red said as she gave him a weak shove. She knew he had done the right thing, they wouldn't have made it otherwise, but she wasn't about to let him off the hook easy either.

"Hey! You know–"

James saw Red's smile and a goofy grin appeared on his face. "Okay, you got me."

Red shook her head again and blinked several times in rapid succession. "Ugh, I am still a bit out of it. How long until Atrus is done?"

James heard a slight beep from under his jacket. "About now." He pulled out the cylindrical device and pushed the button on the bottom.

Atrus flashed on in front of them. He stretched. "I apologize it took so long, but I am now at 100% capacity."

James slipped Atrus back into the lower pocket of his holster and stood up. "I will see about getting us some current clothes."

"We could use Atrus' holograms," Trisia said.

"We could, but at this point I would rather be conservative on his use. We might need the ability more later."

Red nodded. "Agreed. And I need to rest a little more, I think." She slid over and was asleep the second her head touched the floor.

"Watch Red, and if anything odd happens, let me know."

Trisia nodded. "But …umm …what if someone comes in here? I can't exactly give them a good reason or sneak out with Red under my arm."

James smiled. "I can fix that, I wanted to save its power in case we needed it later, but you're right we can't have anyone walking in on you." James reached in his bag and pulled out the Shell, powered it on, it floated off of his hand and several feet into the air. "There, if anyone comes in Atrus can stun them."

Trisia smiled. "Thank you."

James slung the bag back over his shoulder and stood making a sweeping motion over his body. "Atrus, how about something a little more in fashion with the time, please?"

Atrus nodded. "As you wish." His image flickered and disappeared.

James' clothes morphed and shifted into a long tunic extending almost to his ankles. A belt around his waist held the whole thing together. "I'll be back as soon as I can."

He opened the door on the house and stepped out into late evening air. The stench was more oppressive than before as the discarded remnants, heated all day by the hot sun, continued to release their noxious odors. James' nose wrinkled, but he tried not to. The people here would be used to it and standing out is one thing he couldn't afford.

He walked up and down the dirt streets looking for a source

of clothing, but nothing looked apparent. "Atrus?" James whispered, "Where is the market? Perhaps I can buy some."

"With what, Sir?" Atrus whispered back. "You don't have any medium of exchange that would work in this time."

"Perhaps I could locate a few coins then?"

"That would not be probable. While Babylonians did have the shekel, its use was not common."

"How could they have money but not use it in their marketplace? It doesn't make sense."

"The Babylonians used the silver shekel more often as a weight reference of exchange rather than actual use of coinage. Many people were paid in barley or other commodities, using the shekel to set the value."

"Ah trade at it's simplest. And since I have nothing to trade, time to switch to another plan."

"Which is?"

"We borrow them." James continued walking and turned towards the far corner along the city wall where the population seemed less active. "Atrus? Is anyone at home?"

"Yes, in the right section of the house, just off of the interior courtyard, in the kitchen area. A female slave preparing dinner from what I can determine."

"The Kitchen? This should work. Activate the holographic cloak."

"May I remind you, that will take a lot more energy."

"I know, it can't be helped."

James watched as his hand and arm became transparent. He opened the front door with great care not to make a sound and slipped inside. He made his way through several rooms, into the courtyard, then took a left towards the bedrooms. Along the back wall he hit the jackpot. A terra cotta chest containing several tunics, belts, and sandals. He grabbed three sets, closed the chest, and slipped back out.

James breathed a sigh of relief even amongst the assault to his nostrils, then held it again as a man walked past but didn't seem to notice the door opening and closing with no one stepping through. After he was gone, James breathed again. "That was close. I thought for sure I heard someone about to come out of the kitchen. Or that guy noticed the door opening and closing." James shimmered back as Atrus disabled the cloak and regenerated the Babylonia clothing.

"You did hear the cook heading towards you. I created a holographic bug to land on the food she was preparing. It returned her attention to the job at hand," Atrus said.

"Well done."

"Thank you, Sir."

James made his way back to Red and Trisia. By the time he reached them, daylight was almost gone. He made sure no one was in the area, entered the house, and barred the door. He poked his head around the corner and smiled at Red and Trisia. "Anyone here order a tunic?"

"You're back! I started to wonder if something happened," Trisia said, blinking in the dim light.

"It took me a while to find something suitable. I didn't exactly have Babylonian money."

"Sir, I told you Bab–"

"Never mind Atrus. And a little light please. Something suitable for the time." The room lit up and flickered as several small cup-shaped oil lamps appeared in the room.

James held out a tunic, and Trisia grabbed it. She slipped it on but realized she would have to remove her jeans as the cuffs stuck out at the bottom. She stepped into one of the adjoining rooms and removed her jeans, returning holding them out. "What do I do with these?"

"I'll take them." James held out his hand, and Trisia placed them in his grasp. He took off his bag, unzipped it, and stuffed the pants inside.

"What do I do for shoes? I assume sneakers won't exactly fit in here." She looked down at the shoes on her feet with its mix of black, white, and turquoise coloring.

James held out one pair of sandals he had found. "Here."

"You have got to be kidding! You except me to wear sandals through that garbage heap out there? Ick!"

"Just don't walk through anything. There is enough room from what I saw."

"Be thankful they have recently clayed the streets," Atrus said.

Trisia blinked. "Clayed the streets?"

"The Babylonians put a fresh layer of clay down over the trash instead of removing it, once it got to be excessive."

"That's crazy," Trisia said.

"No kidding. I assume it is why disease ran rampant throughout early cities?" James asked.

"Quite correct," Atrus said.

Trisia took off her tricolored sneakers, white socks, and handed them to James who stuffed them into his bag. She slipped on the sandals and frowned. "They don't exactly fit."

"Well, if you tie them on, they won't fall off. Mine don't fit that well either. I suspect they had only one or two sizes at this point."

In the corner Red stirred and sat up. "Got anything for me?"

"Red! Your awake," James said.

"Naturally I am, did you really think I could sleep through you two talking?"

"We weren't loud."

"Oh, hush and give me one of those tunics." She held out her hand.

James tossed one over, she slipped her head through the hole, wrapped it around herself, and tied it in place with the belt James threw over.

Trisia pointed to Red's full-length bodysuit peeking out from under the tunic. "I don't think that is going to work."

Red smiled. "Oh, it will." She reached under the tunic, moved the zipper along both legs up and rolled them out of sight. "There, no one will see them now."

"Won't it be hot?"

"Nope, this fabric breathes almost like a second skin."

"Amazing stuff, holds up to her speed, keeps her cool and breathes as well," James said. He heard Red's stomach rumble. He smiled, reached into his bag, and tossed her an energy bar. "Can't have you hungry."

She caught it mid-air and smiled back. "Thanks, I didn't realize I was hungry until now."

"Do we go out and try to find my Father tonight?"

"I would advise against it; in this time, people refrained from much activity at night unless there was a specific need. Often such a need was of a criminal nature," Atrus said.

"He's right. If we go looking around, we will be noticed. We haven't been so far, and I want to keep it that way," Red said.

James sat down on the brick floor. "Time to get comfortable."

Trisia sighed. "Yeah, right. Brick is never comfortable."

"It could be worse."

"How?"

"Well, let's see, be chased by dinosaurs, tried and held to be executed by a pharaoh, almost have your head taken off by a cannon, Red and I have quite the list."

Red laughed. "That we do. And my list is even longer."

Trisia turned. "Why is that?"

"Because I was doing this for quite a while before James and I met."

James slid over next to Red, rubbing shoulders with her. "And now you wouldn't think of jumping without me."

Red smirked and shoved at his shoulder with her own. "Don't push your luck."

"Atrus kill the light. Might as well save the power while we rest."

The lights vanished. "And did you wish to disable the Shell as well?" Atrus said.

"No, leave it out for now. Should anyone come knocking, you can take care of them."

"Acknowledged," Atrus said. The Shell floated towards the small hallway near the entrance and Atrus lowered it to the floor to save power.

In the darkness James felt Red's head rest against his shoulder as she fell asleep.

Light streamed into the room from the courtyard and James opened one eye. Trisia lay at his left side spread out along the wall, and Red was still resting against his shoulder. He moved a little, Red stirred and opened her eyes, squinting. She sat up and stretched. "Morning already? I didn't think I would sleep through the night."

Trisia wiggled and sat up. "Ugh, worst night I ever had. Every point on my body hurts."

James smiled. "We've had worse. One time–"

Trisia grunted as she held up her hands. "Never mind, I'm sure you have. But this is all new to me." She stood up and stumbled a bit from stiff joints.

The Shell hovered into the room. "Atrus? Anything in the night?" James said.

"Nothing of any consequence. I eliminated one rodent approaching the area."

James sighed. "You shouldn't have wasted the power."

"Speak for yourself!" Trisia said. "I don't want any mice around me, especially when I'm sleeping! I had enough of that in my old lab!"

"It was larger than that," Atrus said.

Trisia hopped around checking the floor. "Eeek! Not again! Where is it?"

"The Shell incinerated it. It will not be an issue, as I said."

Trisia let out a long breath, leaned against the wall as her eyes drifted up towards the ceiling. "Thank you, Atrus."

James' eyes narrowed. "Atrus?"

"Yes, Sir?"

"You wasted power incarcerating a rat?"

"The term wasted is debatable. I expended the energy to do so, yes."

Trisia glared. "He didn't waste it! Red? A little help here."

"I have to admit, I do not wish to have a possible incident with a large rat while I'm trying to sleep on the floor," Red said.

"See? And if you tell him not to do it again, I'm going to kick you in the shins," Trisia said.

James looked at Red's face, then Trisia's and made the only decision he could. "Nice work Atrus."

"Thank you, Sir."

Red leaned over to James' ear. "Smart."

"Like I had a choice," he said out the corner of his mouth.

James stood up and stretched, offering his hand to help Red up. She took it and they both stretched again. "Sanford has to be up and going by now. Let's move," Red said.

"What are we going to do with the bag?" Trisia pointed to the black backpack slung over James' shoulder. "I assume we can't be seen carrying that around?"

"Nope. I found a small cavity behind several loose bricks on the back wall of a storeroom next to the courtyard. I will stick it in there. It will be safe enough for a few days."

James stashed the bag and instructed Atrus to cloak the Shell, sending it over the buildings heading northwest, while they went west, hoping it would speed their efforts to find Sanford.

Red pointed to a street leading off to the right. "This way."

"You seem to know your way around. You didn't even ask Atrus," James said.

"I don't need to. I have been here before."

Trisia blinked. "Wait, what? What do you mean you have been here before?"

James sighed. "Just what she said. She has been here before."

"It was a while ago, but I remember it like it was yesterday. I only stayed a few days to rest on my way to the target temporal zone, and it was this year. It could have been in May, they were harvesting at the time, meaning it was either May or June."

"Great, another problem," James said.

"Why is it a problem?"

"Because, I can't meet up with my previous self without causing a big paradox. And if Sanford–."

"Sees you, he might come after you and your previous self would not understand the danger," Trisia finished for her.

Red nodded. "Exactly. Babylon is a big city, so it is possible he won't bump into my previous self. I kept a low profile and just passed through."

James gritted his teeth. "But it is also possible he might."

Red sighed. "Yes."

"Do you remember where you were?" Trisia asked.

"Most of the time I stayed near the Ishtar gate and Processional Way. There are markets along the street and it was easy to blend in. At night, I found a quiet corner and stayed there. Like I said, I was only here a couple of days."

"Sounds like he won't see you then," Trisia said.

"I moved around a little if someone had a suspicious look when they saw me. But it didn't happen often. Most of the people here kept to themselves."

James' eyes flashed. "Atrus? Can you detect Sanford if he is using his new cloak?"

"It is possible, it would depend on if he is disturbing the ground he is walking on. Even if he is not disrupting the dirt, he might leave a slight change in temperature as he walks over the hot street."

James looked at Trisia as they continued walking. "Any idea where he might go?"

"I don't know, this is a bit out of my league," Trisia said.

"Then I shall profile him, he is a terrorist trying to make as much damage as possible." James turned and pointed to the one massive building dominating the skyline. "For this time period that would be the ziggurat I see reaching up from the horizon."

"The building in question is the Etemenanki, or the 'temple of the foundation of heaven and earth' as the Babylonians called it. Or to be more specific, it is a temple dedicated to Marduk," Atrus whispered.

"Thanks Atrus, but whatever its use, it would appear to be the most significant place here. Not to mention when destroyed it will send material everywhere, increasing the damage over all."

"I don't think it would make much difference if he has several of those modified power cells," Trisia said.

"Perhaps not, but I still think he would see it as a large target. Atrus, the Shell is heading in the general direction correct?"

"Yes, Sir," Atrus whispered.

"Good, center your search on the base and the area around the ziggurat. I suspect the enclosure would be under less scrutiny than the temple itself."

"Very logical. I will center my observations to the enclosure area. Also, my data indicates several of the buildings on the side closest to us of the enclosure were for grain storage."

Red smiled. "Bingo. They will fill them in a straight line. Check the farthest one."

Red, James, and Trisia quickened their pace down the road and they almost bumped into several Babylonians along the way. After another block, Atrus beeped.

"I have visual confirmation," Atrus said.

"Where?" James said.

"Next to the last storage building going from south to north. He has left and reactivated his cloak, but I am still able to follow."

"Good. Continue following him while we check out that building," Red said.

They moved as fast as they dared, trying not to attract attention, and sneaked past the guards at one of enclosure entrances with relative ease. Apparently, they didn't take their job too seriously with a penalty of death to anyone violating the sacred spaces.

When they reached the small storage building Atrus beeped again. "I detect someone inside."

"Who?" James said.

"Oh no," Red said, "this is not good."

"Affirmative it is Red's earlier self. I have detected trace amounts of Red's unique bodysuit fabric along one side of the door frame."

Red's face scrunched up. "I did wear it under a long shawl when I was here."

Trisia looked around the corner, then back. "Wait? If the person in there is you, shouldn't you remember this?"

"It could be when we traveled through time, jumped at the edge of the temporal storm, and arrived before Sanford is allowing me to exist outside of the normal influences. This only a guess, as I have never done it. And hoped I never would."

"So now what do we do?" Trisia said.

They both looked at her. "You go in and rescue me," Red said.

"What? Me? Why me?"

"Because I never saw you until recently. If I recognize you when we meet the first time, it won't be much of a problem since we don't have a large time-line at that point. Compared to if I realize who James is when I meet him and it alters what I would have done in some way."

"Couldn't you wear one of Atrus' holograms?"

James sighed. "She knows me too well. My movements, what I would say, and how I say it. And naturally, herself even more so. You on the other hand, she wouldn't notice those details when you two meet for the first time. Or at least it is not near as likely."

"Okay okay, I get the point. I will go rescue the earlier you," Trisia sighed.

Trisia took two steps before James said, "Wait."

She looked back. "What?"

"No sense in taking chances. Atrus, a little disguise please."

Trisia blinked as her arm changed to a darker color and her face took on a more local Babylonian image. Her tunic even changed color. "Wow, even though I have seen it many times, this still blows my mind."

James smiled and held up a finger. "Remember not to speak. She might figure out you are not Babylonian."

"What am I supposed to do when she says something?"

"Simple, use hand motions. She will follow, then you lose her in the crowd."

Trisia put her hands on her hips. "And how am I supposed to do that? She can run light years faster than me."

"Lead her towards the Ishtar gate, then take a quick right after you pass a side street, let us know and Atrus will change your look. Then you can disappear easy enough."

Trisia sighed. "Right. Okay, here goes." She slipped around the corner and up the steps to the door. It had a bar across it, but she pushed it out of the way and pulled the door open. Inside the unlit room a woman blinked. Trisia walked over and untied the woman's wrists, then pointed towards the door. A red head bobbed, and she followed. James and Red saw the two of them exit the building, close the door behind them, and head towards the gates.

"Atrus? Do you still have a lock on Sanford?" James asked.

"Affirmative. He is on the other side of the Etemenanki."

"What is he doing?"

"Placing power cells around its base. Your assumption of his plan seems to be correct."

"How many has he placed?"

"One. He is now placing a second."

"Keep a lock on him. Trisia? How are you doing?"

"Mm-hmm," Trisia said as he continued to head towards the main gates with the early Red right behind her.

"I assume her expression means she is heading towards the primary gates with the earlier Red," Atrus said.

James rolled his eyes as he ran in the opposite direction. "Obviously that is what it means. Red? Can you see them yet? I'm heading after Sanford."

Red ran down a parallel street covering the distance in under two seconds. She peaked out from her vantage point near the city gates. "Yes, I see me and Trisia. They are almost here. But the other me is too close; she won't be able to head down the street before I will see her. Change of plan. Trisia, there is a small recessed area to your right before the gates. It is behind the meat and clothing seller. Do you see them?"

"Mm-hmm." Came a quiet reply.

"Good, take a few more steps and stay put. I will tell you when," Red said. She watched carefully, took several steps down the street and pushed on one of the poles holding up a seller's tent. It started leaning, and she returned to her previous hidden location.

The large pole stretched at the fabric holding it in place until it could not take the strain anymore. It ripped and fell over, pulling the tent down with it, which pulled the tent down next to it. This continued in a domino effect, overturning different merchant's stalls. People struggled to get out from under the fabric to see what had happened. The crowd swelled with curious onlookers. "*Now*," Red said.

While earlier Red watched the ensuing chaos Trisia slipped behind one of the still-standing tents and into a hidden recessed area along the wall. "I'm in place," she whispered.

"Understood, changing your appearance," Atrus said.

Trisia watched as her skin lightened, hair darkened, and the tunic she wore shifted to a lighter shade of blue. She smiled and stepped out. Earlier Red's head swiveled around looking for her as the different merchants pointed fingers at each other shouting insults.

Trisia walked away from the market and headed towards the ziggurat. Earlier Red did not follow. "I'm clear."

"She is. I'm baffled and heading in the opposite direction. It worked," Red said.

20

Red watched herself disappear into the crowd. "Atrus where is Sanford?"

"Near the ziggurat, northeast corner. James is en route."

Red's eyes narrowed. "Atrus, how are you tracking him? Is he making that much of a trail in the dirt?"

"Negative. While I could also track him through infrared and other minute changes as he walks across the ground, it is unnecessary. I can see him clearly," Atrus said.

Red blinked. "Why doesn't he have his cloak on? Something is not right."

"I would assume to save power, it does require a lot of energy."

"Yes, it does. But he has the power cells now, it should have enough to place the ones he wants to explode and still remain cloaked, don't you think?"

Atrus would have shrugged if his hologram were active. "Possible, but we do not know how much the device has been used or its capacity."

Red leaned against the brick wall while her eyes drifted up towards the ziggurat. "I know, it must take a lot. But if I were him, I would still want to stay hidden as much as possible."

Trisia continued walking back from the gates towards the

ziggurat and its wall enclosure, thankful this road wasn't full of garbage. "I agree, he wouldn't take the risk unless he had to."

"Which is essentially what I stated," Atrus said.

James slipped past the guards again and raced along the southern enclosure wall. "Will you two knock it off. It doesn't matter why is he visible. We are going to take him down. Atrus, can you get a clear shot without triggering any power cells he is carrying?"

"Yes I can, I have determined unless a direct energy impact occurs, the devices will remain stable. However, you neglected to ask if such a shot would be seen. And I regret to inform you it will. There are several priests nearby."

James moved across the space to the inner wall and a nearby building, advancing on Sanford's position. His head jacked around a corner and back again. "Can you get it into a position so it won't?"

"Negative. If I move it into a position where it won't be seen, it will be unable to take the shot you wanted," Atrus said.

"Then I will take care of this myself." James' head popped around the corner and he smiled pulling the weapon from the holster under his tunic, opened the grip, entered a configuration code for stealth mode on the touchpad, closed the grip, and took aim. "I can take him from here."

Red leaned forward as her hand touched the earpiece. "James! No! Atrus said there are priests nearby. You can't!" Red said.

"We don't have a choice! If he activates that power cell, I'm sure they will go off in a few seconds. He won't make the same mistake again by having a long countdown. I can't let him activate it. I turned on the stealth system, the chances anyone will see anything is almost nil." James raised the energy pistol and tapped the trigger. A red bead lit up in the sight, showing he had a lock on Sanford's head.

"James! No! I will get him!" Before he could blink, Red put on a tremendous burst of speed and appeared right next to Sanford. Feeling the wind from her quick approach, he turned and grinned.

Red's eyes went wide, and they both disappeared.

"Atrus! What happened? Where did they go?" James said.

"I do not know."

"I thought you said you could track Sanford even if cloaked!"

"Sir, I can. However, this location is now in the shadow of the ziggurat. I cannot track through thermal changes in that area, and he did not leave any other traces on the hard ground as he often does."

James squinted and used the sight on the energy pistol, scanning the area. "I don't see the power cell."

"I do not detect it either. Sanford must have taken it."

James crossed the space between the inner west wall and the ziggurat for a better look. Trisia snuck past the guards at the ziggurat enclosure wall and raced towards James. "What about the other one? You said he had one in position?" Her words came out in breathless gasps.

"Affirmative. That one has disappeared as well," Atrus said.

James gritted his teeth. "Or he never placed it."

Trisia reached James breathing hard, stopped, and bent over trying to catch her breath. After a few seconds, her head popped up. "What? Atrus saw him place it."

"Correct, I did."

James shook his head. "No, you didn't. You only thought you did. This was all a trap. He wanted to capture Red."

"But Sir, I did see him place a device."

"And was that done with him cloaked?"

"Negative, he was visible at the time."

"And was there a moment where the Shell did not have him in clear view?"

"Affirmative, when he was moving around the southeast corner of the ziggurat," Atrus said.

James nodded. "He turned on the cloak and back tracked when you were moving the Shell into a different position. I bet if he ran, he could grab the device and return before you realized."

Atrus paused for several seconds. "It is possible but not probable."

Trisia leaned up against the fired brick of the ziggurat and sighed. "It's not your fault Atrus, he fooled us all."

James' eyes went wide as he slapped his forehead. "Atrus shouldn't you be able to track Red's earpiece?"

"Yes Sir, but I cannot detect any signal from it," Atrus said.

Trisia cocked her head. "Did she lose it?"

"Negative. If she lost the device, I would still be able to track it. I am detecting nothing."

James sighed as his eyes drifted towards the sky, and he leaned against the ziggurat. "Just great. Sanford's cloak can block its signal."

"Unfortunately, that appears to be the case, Sir," Atrus said.

"What do we do?" Trisia asked.

James poked his head around the corner and whipped back. Two priests had come down the ziggurat's steps and were heading towards the southeast section of the enclosure. "We stay out of sight and wait. Not much else we can do," James said.

Red tried to move but found she couldn't. It felt like she was watching someone else far away through a TV display, even though she couldn't actually see anything. She couldn't feel a thing either. Even her eyes refused to move. Not that it would do her much good. The last she remembered she saw Sanford turning with a grin large enough to swallow a planet, and feeling something. Then this...

Suddenly the darkness vanished into a blinding light. For the first time since this happened, she felt pain for a few seconds until her eyes adjusted. They focused on a form standing in front of her. When they finished, she wished for the blackness. Linus Sanford still had *that* grin.

"There my dear, isn't that better without the hood? I didn't want to take the chance you could communicate our position before we got here, however unlikely that might be."

Red glared. She couldn't do anything else.

"I bet you are wondering what happened? Well, I knew you would come after me, but I changed the game by setting up a little trap I knew you couldn't resist."

Red's eyes quivered, and she wished she could do more. Anything at all.

"Ah, I saw that. Good. You are in there and conscious. This wouldn't be any fun otherwise."

Her eyes quivered again.

"I bet you are wondering what happened? Oh, right I already said that." He leaned close enough for her to smell onions on his breath. "Well, I can't help it." He grinned again and Red wished she could spit in his eye.

Sanford straightened and took several steps back. Red could see she was in another building similar to the one her previous self was in before. Although this one looked a little different with a much larger window. He leaned against the mud-brick wall. "Where was I? Oh yes what happened. You see, I have developed a drug which can freeze a target in place without damaging them. They stay fully conscious and aware but are unable to move. I know you have seen it before. But this is a very special batch I made just for you. I know your metabolism is faster than a normal person's and would burn through my little invention in no time at all otherwise. Your counterpart did after all, even with a few adjustments."

Sanford paused to look out the window. Seeing nothing of interest, he turned back. "However, I didn't have a proper lab to calibrate it, and it was pure guesswork." He walked over and lowered down to his haunches. "It would appear my guesses were correct. This will keep you out of the way until I finish what I started. And your friends will be too busy trying to find you, to stop me."

He stood back up, walked over to the door, pulled it open, and the increased light whitewashed her vision for several seconds until her eyes could compensate. Sanford turned back. "By the way, your unusual metabolism has had an unexpected reaction to this version of my compound. While it created the desired response, your body seems unable to deal with it and is slowly shutting down. By my estimates you will be dead in less than an hour."

Red's eyes quivered again.

"Nope, I'm not worried about killing you. While I would like to study you more, there isn't much point. I have the data I need, not that I can make use of it now due to your interference. But once I'm done, it won't matter anyway. I'm about to make the biggest change in history and you will have a front-row seat! Well, if you live that long. And you might be wondering how I plan on surviving the temporal changes? Simple. I will open a dimensional portal a second before it hits. I will exist outside of time at that moment exiting right after and with my technology I will appear as a god! I will control what is left of humanity with ease! But for now I must bid you adieu." He cocked his hand in a one fingered salute and closed the door. She heard something else, a bit of pounding, and all was quiet.

"Sir, I detect Miss Red's A.T.E. It would appear the interference has abated." Atrus said.

"Her earpiece? Where?" James stood up and brushed the dirt from his tunic. He and Trisia had moved several times in the past hour, trying to stay out of sight. James poked his head around the corner. Another pair of priests approached but from the opposite direction and headed up the stairs of the ziggurat.

"In the–"

Trisia stood up. "About time. Where did he take her?"

Atrus paused. "As I was about to say, in the newer section of the city across the river. Northwest of our current position."

Trisia blinked. "How did he get over there so fast?"

"The dimensional door, I would assume," James said.

"Negative Sir. It would put a drain on his energy reserves and increase the time before he could utilize the power cells at full capacity. Not to mention creating the door is a visible affair, and he wouldn't want to be seen," Atrus said.

James pointed towards one of the enclosure gates and Trisia followed. The guards weren't watching the far entrance, and they slipped past without incident. They walked down the street and towards the river. The sun glinted off the calm water. "Now what? We can't swim," James said.

"Well, I can if we need," Trisia said.

"Not that far. And I don't want you worn out when you get there anyway."

"There is the Euphrates tunnel, Sir," Atrus stated.

"The what?"

"It is a tunnel under the river. It connects between the palace on this side of the river to a temple on the west side. While there is a bridge across the Euphrates south and left of our position, this will reach Miss Red with increased speed."

James sighed. "Thanks Atrus, but I don't know how we could use it. Won't access be restricted?"

"Possible, but it was built by Semiramis. At this point in time, its use is more widespread for merchants or those moving goods between different areas of the city."

Trisia bit her bottom lip. "We don't exactly look like merchants."

James rubbed his chin. "While we might be able to fake it given time, we don't have the luxury. Atrus, do you have enough power to cloak us both?"

"I do have enough to get you both over there. Back again, might be more problematic."

"We will tackle that bridge when we get to it."

Trisia smiled. "Don't you mean Tunnel?"

James laughed. "Okay, tunnel. Atrus? Which way?"

"To your right. The entrance is on the bank, outside the palace wall," Atrus said.

"At least we won't have to get past the palace guards," James said as they approached the river bank. In the distance he could see people entering what looked like a twelve by fifteen-foot wide cave at the edge of the river. "That must be it. Atrus, do your stuff."

Trisia's eyes drifted down in time to see her hand disappear along with the rest of her. "This is wild. How do I know where to put my feet?"

"Walk carefully. And try not to move too fast or Atrus will have problems keeping you invisible."

"I know, I remember him telling you that before."

They continued on and after a few minutes walked right past the guards and entered the Euphrates tunnel. Bricks lined the passage and every two or three meters a lit oil lamp drove away the darkness. It wasn't a lot of light, but enough to see where the walls were and if any of the bricks lining the floor had raised up enough to grab at their elevated sandals.

It was surprisingly dry within the tunnel and Trisia couldn't help reaching out to feel the wall. Cool to the touch, but not damp at all. "How do they keep this so dry when it is under a river?" she whispered. "It's a challenge in our time."

"Bitumen," Atrus said.

"Bit-umen? What in the world is that?"

James cracked a grin even though Trisia couldn't see it. "Asphalt. It's the black stuff you see peeking out between the bricks."

"Quite correct Sir. Bitumen is the word used in this time. The area is rich in the resource and how they built such large wonders. Several of these technological advances won't occur again for thousands of years," Atrus whispered in their earpieces.

Merchants passed them on the other side of the tunnel, pushing carts or drawn by animals. They carried everything from wine, to clothes, and even meat. James and Trisia kept out of the way and moved as fast as the cloak would allow. Nine-hundred twenty-nine meters later they emerged into the sunlight and hustled past lion statues, several priests, and out of the temple. Outside, James leaned up against the wall. "I don't see anyone. Drop the cloaks."

"Affirmative," Atrus said as the holograms abated, revealing themselves once again.

"I hope we don't have to do that again. It's too weird," Trisia said.

"It takes some getting used to, I admit," James said. "Atrus, where to now?"

"Take the street to your North and right, up two sections, then turn left. There is a house on the corner. Red is located in an area farthest from the front door on the right side of the house."

James stopped. "What? Why is she there?"

Trisia stopped and turned. "What do you mean?"

"Why would Sanford take her there? It makes little sense."

"Obviously he thinks we can't find her there."

"Maybe, or maybe he is trying to keep us away from what he is planning. Atrus, send the Shell back to the ziggurat. I have a hunch Sanford will show up soon."

"Affirmative, Sir," Atrus replied. The floating still-invisible device, which had been following them, turned around, hovered high in the sky, and headed back towards the ziggurat.

As they approached the house James examined the various

buildings. These were newer and had signs of recent construction. In fact, it felt more like a posh neighborhood. "Atrus, I'm betting the house isn't empty."

"Correct Sir, I was about to mention it. There is a slave in the front kitchen area and one person in the main living room area off of the courtyard."

"Same layout as the house we were in before?"

"Affirmative."

"Then it means Red is in the storage area behind the kitchen?"

"Correct."

James sighed. "We have a problem."

"Why? You go in there while invisible and grab her."

James shook his head. "I can't. Atrus is running low on power."

"I should have enough for that long," Atrus said.

"No, we might need it later. From what I remember, there is not any way I could sneak in past them."

"Correct Sir. Both entrances from the forward kitchen and courtyard are highly visible."

"I guess I'm going to have to do it the old-fashioned way."

Trisia cocked her head. "What way is that?"

"Improvise. Follow me and be quiet."

Trisia nodded as James opened the door open as quietly as he could and then crept inside. The thick six-foot walls were performing their job, blocking the day's heat with the interior feeling much cooler. James turned to his right, took several steps and peeked an eye around the corner. By the counter, next to the wall, a slave ground flour for the daily bread. James pulled his weapon from its holster, popped open the grip, keyed in a sequence and snapped it closed a little louder than he intended.

The slave's head rose up and James noticed how beautiful she was and thought it unusual for a kitchen slave. Her head went back and forth sending her hair in multiple directions looking for the sound. She took two steps towards the inner kitchen. James touched the trigger and an almost silent whine erupted from the barrel followed by an energy bolt a microsecond later. The bolt sailed out and struck the slave while her head was turned. Blue electric arcs raced up and down her body; a second later she went down in a heap.

"That's one," James mouthed. He moved to the other side and stuck the edge of his head around the corner of the courtyard. He saw the other person in the living room. A woman of the household, by the look of her. She wore a lavish tunic with bright colors and sat on a padded lounge. Her eyes stayed focused on the clay tablet she was reading. James touched the trigger again and her head fell backwards, resting on the edge of the lounge. "And that's two."

James flicked a finger towards the kitchen with the slave on the brick floor and placed the weapon back in its holster. "You keep an eye on her and the woman in the living room, I'm going to get Red."

Trisia reached out and grabbed his shoulder. "And what do I do if they wake up?"

James smiled. "Don't worry, they won't wake up until after sunset. By that time we will be long gone."

Trisia folded her arms and grunted. "I hope so. I don't really want to explain what we are doing in their house."

James ran off and found the storage room at the back of the kitchen. He pulled at the door but it refused to budge. "What is wrong with this thing?"

"Sir if you notice there are several shards of broken material wedged in and around the door frame," Atrus said.

James sighed. "I could blast the whole door but Red wouldn't like me leaving a temporal footprint that big if I can avoid it."

"You could try the window," Atrus said.

He smiled. Two steps to the right of the door, a recessed window sat covered with a terra cotta grate. He peeked between the holes in the grate and saw Red. She wasn't moving. "Red I'm coming."

The window was large enough to fit through. He took several steps back and rammed the grate with his shoulder. He stepped back, rubbing his arm and especially his elbow. "Ow! That stuff is stronger than it looks." He could free the door given time, but the thought of what Sanford must be doing turned his stomach. And more importantly, Red wasn't moving. He had to get in there *now*. Reaching for the holstered weapon at his side, he spotted a pole resting next to several of the cooking pots. The far end had an old bent iron spear head jammed on. It must have been used to move the hot coals around when cooking. James smiled, picked it up, took several steps back, and rammed the middle of the terra cotta grate. The iron tip, while bent, channeled all his force into one single point in the center. The grate unable to resist, snapped into four sections, and fell in.

James scrambled through the window. Red lay sitting on the brick floor, her eyes open, unmoving. "Red I'm here. Red?"

Her one eye quivered.

"She is in there. He must have used the same substance on her as the security guards in Russia."

"Correct Sir, hold me out that I might complete a full scan."

James pulled Atrus' cylinder from the pocket on his holster and held it out. A green beam extended out, ran up and down Red several times and retracted. "While the compound used is similar to Russia, there are several differences. One moment…"

Trisia peeked her head in the broken window and pointed to the pieces on the floor. "They aren't going to like this."

James sighed. "I didn't have much choice, I had to get in here. At least I didn't blast or disintegrate the door. And aren't you supposed to be keeping an eye on the people out there?"

"Yeah, well, they aren't going anywhere." She hauled herself through the broken window. "What's wrong with Red?"

Atrus beeped. "I have concluded the chemical used is a different and more potent version from the one utilized in Russia. It is reacting to Red's immune system in a unique way and her body is shutting down. The damage will be irreversible in 48 minutes."

James' hands balled into fists. "Sanford! If he did this, he must have an antidote. Any sign of him at the ziggurat?"

"Not yet, Sir. But if your suspicions are correct, there should be in short order," Atrus said.

James stood up. "You stay with Red. I'm going after Sanford."

"But what if someone else comes home?" Trisia said.

James' eyebrows met. "That could be a problem."

"Sir, it won't be an issue. I read the tablet the lady in the living room was reading. It is a letter from her husband. He won't be back for another week yet."

"Good, and they won't wake up for several hours. We have time." James pointed to Trisia. "Stay here. If need be, you can move her."

Trisia snorted, looking at the taller catatonic woman on the floor. "Great. And how am I going to do that?"

James smiled. "You will think of something."

Trisia folded her arms. "Thanks a heap!"

James scrambled back out the window and ran out of the house. "Atrus, you said you didn't have enough power to cloak us both, do you have enough for me?"

"I should Sir, but it will be close."

"It will have to do." James continued to run but stopped before he reached the entrance to the tunnel. He breathed hard several times, trying to slow his racing heart and breath. "Okay Atrus, activate the cloak."

"Affirmative Sir."

A second later James walked past the guards and down into the tunnel as fast as he could without sounding like an invisible running man. At about the half-way point Atrus beeped in his ear. "Sir, I have detected Sanford. You were correct, he has returned to the ziggurat," Atrus whispered into his earpiece. Atrus perceived a nod. "Yes Sir, I am monitoring. He has not placed any power cells as of this moment. He is cloaked and I'm detecting through thermal variances."

James exited the tunnel, still trying not to breathe hard while moving as fast as he could. When he turned a corner, Atrus dropped the cloak. James ran towards the ziggurat enclosure. "Sir, the third entrance is unattended. But might I suggest you slow down before then or you might draw attention to yourself? Sanford has placed one power cell at the southwest corner of the ziggurat, in the corner at the base of the main steps."

"Noted," James said, breathing hard. He stopped before the gates and walked past, ignoring the guards. They didn't notice him, and he did the same for the next. The third one he slipped in and made his way towards the corner of the ziggurat. "Where is he now?"

"He is above you. Second level of the ziggurat," Atrus said.

James' eyes shot up. "Great, he would decide to go up this time." He saw the lower staircase on the west side and headed for it. He raced up them as best he could, grateful he didn't have to go up the whole thing. His head whipped back and forth. No priests. "Atrus, where is he now?"

"Southwest corner. This level."

James stared at the corner and saw a power cell appear near the edge of the walkway. He pulled the weapon from the holster under his tunic. "You will have to guide me. I can't take the risk he will activate it and leave. He may only have two."

"Understood Sir. But be advised I cannot guide you with 100% certainty."

"I know." He raised the pistol, steadied it in a recessed area in the wall, and aimed towards the power cell.

"To the left Sir, down three degrees. To the right until mark …mark …it's a lock."

James touched the trigger. A narrow, almost imperceptible red beam lashed out and hit an invisible barricade. Sparks raced up and down, growing stronger until the vague silhouette of a man appeared. The silhouette grew stronger until, at last, Sanford shook and staggered backwards. His head whipped back and forth as his hand reached out to touch the brick facade of the ziggurat. He looked down at the panel on his chest. A missing corner flashed with electrical arcs passing between damaged circuits.

James raced towards Sanford and jammed him against the

wall with his left arm, his right hand squeezed, the weapon held inches from the man's nose. "Give me the antidote!"

Sanford's eyes cleared and focused on the man holding him. "Antidote? Oh, you found her eh? Well good for you."

"You have lost. Your device is ruined, and I will disable your bombs. Give me the antidote now, and maybe I won't kill you."

Sanford grinned. "You won't kill me. It's not in you."

James' eyes narrowed. "Do you really want to take that chance?"

Sanford's grin widened. "Don't bluff me. I know you won't take the risk of killing me when I might help that woman."

"That woman? *That* woman? She is the woman I love!" In that instant Sanford saw the fury and rage in James' eyes and realized he had miscalculated. Such a man was capable of anything. "Give me the antidote!"

"Never!"

"Your plan has failed . . . again you have lost, why take Red with you?"

Sanford summoned all of his strength and pushed at James. "Because I can!" James staggered backward, distracted for a microsecond thinking Sanford had no other choice. Sanford's eyes locked on the edge of the ziggurat, and he raced towards it.

James reached out a second too slow. "Don't do it!"

"And do what? Go back with you? Or worse? Never!" He turned and leaped over a low point in the wall and from the building.

Sanford started falling and jabbed at a button on his chest. Arcs of power rippled and flashed but failed to coalesce into a single point as before. "No!" A second later his body collided with the hard ground, making a dull thud.

James shook his head and leaned over the edge, looking down at the mess of disjointed limbs. "It's finally over," but as he said it he winced realizing the same was true for Red. James opened his eyes and thought he saw a spark. He blinked and several more sparks appeared and started to rake Sanford's body over and over again. In a brilliant flash, an orb of white-hot energy appeared in the middle of his body, expanded growing hotter and brighter by the second until it enveloped him, flashed again and disappeared. James stood looking at the two-meter spherical hole in the dirt where a man had been seconds before. "Atrus? What was that?"

"Implosion. Hard to tell for certain without a detailed analysis of his equipment."

"Good luck on that, considering nothing is left."

"Quite true Sir."

"Is it possible …" Trisia's wavering voice came through James' earpiece.

"Negative. Based on the data we have of his technology and what I have just observed, a full implosion took place. Nothing known could have survived," Atrus stated.

A tear slipped down Trisia's cheek. "I've always known. While I had hope, I also knew he would never stop. He was a difficult man to begin with. But with his condition …"

"May I suggest we disable the power cells and leave before someone comes looking?" Atrus said.

Trisia brushed away the tears with a quick swipe of her hand. "I agree, since we don't want to get blasted either."

"Don't worry, I can disable them," James said. He took several steps to his left and knelt down to the power cell at his feet. Pulling a screw driver from under his tunic he removed the cover and pulled the middle circuit board as before. But the lit display didn't shut down. "Umm Atrus? Why isn't this shutting down?"

A green beam lashed out from beneath his tunic and retracted. "Sanford has attached a small capacitor which is continuing to power the circuitry and will last longer than we have time for. If you short the connection B3 to W1 it will activate a power saving measure and shunt the power back into the cell."

James' eyebrow raised. "Can it take that kind of power feedback?"

"Professor Keleeigan incorporated a lot of safeguards and over-engineered the system. Sanford did not remove all of them; it will accept the excess energy with ease."

"Where is this contact point?"

"Middle section, on the right, next to the power connection port," Atrus said.

James looked at the screwdriver and point between the two contacts. "This is too big I will short something else instead." The power cell began to glow brighter. "Oh, wait a sec." James whipped off the copper safety pin from his tunic and flipped out the long metal shank. He lowered it and first touched B3, then extended it to contact the W1 solder point. The power cell's glow increased for another half second before diminishing.

James slapped the cover back on. "One down." He tucked the power cell under his arm and raced down the steps to the other device at the base. It had already begun to glow brighter than the first.

"I estimate one minute fifty seconds until critical mass," Atrus said.

James jabbed the screwdriver into the slot and cranked. "You aren't helping Atrus."

"You always told me you wanted detailed information, Sir," Atrus said.

"Atrus you aren't helping," Trisia said.

"Very well. Less time now until critical mass."

"That isn't what we meant!" Trisia said.

James pulled off the cover, yanked out the circuit board, and jabbed the pin into the contact point. The power cell flashed brighter, then dimmed. "Whew, that's two." He tucked the other device under his arm. "Trisia, how is Red?"

"No change. If anything, her heart rate is a little slower. Hard for me to tell though."

"I'm headed back. Atrus, how long does she have left?"

"Approximately twenty-eight minutes," Atrus said.

James made his way from the ziggurat back to the tunnel. He stood out of sight, looking at the people entering. "Can you get me through the tunnel again?"

"Perhaps, if I reduce the cloak accuracy while inside the tunnel itself."

James sighed. "We have to take the risk. Do it."

"Very well Sir," Atrus said as the holographic cloak engaged and James disappeared.

He moved fast, causing blur lines as he raced past the guards. "Hey did you see that?"

The other guard blinked. "See what?"

"The wall appeared to move."

"You have been out in the sun too long. It must have been a bug or something. If I were you, I would keep my mouth shut."

The guard chuckled. "Yeah, you're right."

James raced for the other end and Atrus reduced the hologram cloak to almost the point of visibility, but in the dark tunnel no one noticed anything other than wondering where the sudden air movement came from as he raced past. This time the noise of several horses covered the sounds of him running.

James exited the tunnel as fast as he could with the cloak flickering several times. Thankfully the guards were helping a merchant with his overturned cart and failed to notice. Atrus dropped the cloak as soon as he was out of sight. He leaned up against the nearest building, his breath coming in ragged gasps, and his heart still racing. "I hope I never have to do that again. Trisia? We're almost there."

"James, hurry! She isn't good at all."

21

James didn't know where he found the strength to run in the hard, unforgiving sandals for the next three blocks, but he did. He pushed open the front door, secured it, and raced towards the back. The Shell, which had followed him back from the ziggurat, decloaked and moved into the kitchen.

He found the storage room door open and Trisia holding Red's hand. She heard his approach and looked up. "I got tired of crawling through the window, so I used that metal-tipped pole to pry out the little bits holding the door shut." Trisia's head turned back towards Red. "She isn't good. Her pulse is even weaker. And I can't get her to move her eyes like she did before."

James tossed the power cells to Trisia, bent over all out of breath, and collapsed next to Red. He took her hand. "Red? I'm here."

No response.

"I'm truly sorry I got you two into this mess. If it wasn't for me, my Father wouldn't have come back and you–"

James raised his other hand. "Don't worry about it. We don't blame you. You may have started the situation, but you didn't realize your Father was insane. He lied and used you like everyone else."

Trisia leaned back against the cool wall and placed the devices on the floor. "I know, but I still feel like it is all my fault."

"You have helped us and tried to fix the damage. No one could ask for more under the circumstances. And trust me when I say Red feels the same way."

"But I–"

Atrus beeped.

"What is it, Atrus?" James said. In the distance a huge rumble of thunder groaned, then a loud crack, and an even louder rumble. This time it reverberated deep into their bones as it traveled through the ground.

"What was *that*?" Trisia said.

"I have detected a–"

A squeal of static erupted their earpieces causing them to jump. "Testing …one …two …three …testing. James? Do you hear me?"

James blinked. "Doc? Is that you?"

"Who else?"

"No, I mean how are you talking to us?"

"Well Atrus gave me the underlying technology of your A.T.E. earpieces. Quite ingenious actually, wish I had invented them myself."

"No, I mean how are you talking to us through time?"

"He's not. I tried to tell you I detected a temporal event," Atrus said.

"Doc? You are here?"

"Naturally! Didn't think I could let you have all the fun, do you?"

"How?"

Keleeigan laughed. "My boy Atrus transmitted what was happening the second he detected the approaching temporal event. Luckily, I was at the lighthouse and had just got the equipment installed when he messaged. It took me a little longer to get here than I planned, my temporal coordinates were thrown off jumping without the proper calculations."

"But won't everyone see your lighthouse land?"

"Nope! I modified the temporal field to incorporate Sanford's cloak. Using a low energy temporal field makes the cloak just as powerful, but without the side effects he suffered. No one will know I'm here unless they bump into the building."

"Doc, where are you?"

"Southeast of the city. Just head in this direction, I will come out and show you when you get close."

"Doc, we have a problem. Red is dying."

Keleeigan's eyes went wide. "What happened?"

"Sanford shot her with the same drug he used on the guards in Russia, but this is different."

"Yes, it is a stronger formulation," Atrus added.

Keleeigan reached across his table, picked up a bottle, and checked it for damage. "Well, it is a good thing I brought an antidote."

"What? How?"

"I sent him detailed information from my scans when we returned from Russia," Atrus said.

"That he did, and I finished a counter agent while en route. Had a hunch you might need it. But I don't know if it will work against this formulation. It might not be potent enough."

"We have to try! But I can't be seen carrying her through the city streets; it would bring up too many questions and slow us down."

"Sir, I can send the Shell to pick it up and bring it here. It can travel faster than you carrying Red. But someone will have to open the door to the street, unless you want me to vaporize it."

Trisia chuckled. "No, I will get the door." She stood up and headed towards the front door.

"Do it. Doc, did you hear?"

"I heard. I'll be on the lookout for it."

Trisia saw the Shell hovering by the front door. She grabbed the iron latch, lifted it and pulled the heavy door open. The Shell shimmered and disappeared as it re-cloaked, hovering out into the street. Trisia peeked out, her head swiveling back and forth. She saw the usual filth, but no one even saw her open the door, much less the Shell leave before it was fully cloaked. She closed the door, latched it, and headed back to the storage room. "It's away."

Atrus would have smiled if he could have spared the power for his hologram. "I already told him."

The Shell took off and hovered high above the city, shielded in its cloak as it headed south. It cruised along, heading out of the city as fast as the cloak would allow, but not finding any sign of Keleeigan after several minutes of searching.

"Professor Keleeigan is not detectable, I am lowering the Shell and dropping its cloak," Atrus said.

"Are you sure it can't be seen?" James asked.

"Affirmative, however, I still do not detect Professor Keleeigan." Atrus generated a hologram of the surrounding area for them to see.

They heard a whistle emanating from their earpieces. "Over here." The Atrus rotated the Shell and an older man wearing a white lab coat appeared from nowhere. "Here," Keleeigan said waving his arm and turned to go back the way he came.

The Shell approached and followed Keleeigan. A second later the interior of the lighthouse appeared. "Very impressive Doc," James said.

"Isn't it? I figured it would come in handy." He produced a syringe from the pocket of his lab coat, filled it with fluid and the tightly capped the needle. "Now how do I give this to you? I don't see any hands on this thing."

James chuckled. "Oh right, I forgot I didn't attach them. Doc, hold out your hand."

Keleeigan's right eyebrow raised. "That sounds ominous."

"Trust me, Doc," James said.

"Oh, I do my boy, I do." Keleeigan held out his hand and the Shell lowered, landing in his palm.

"Now Doc, underneath and towards the back there is a tiny button you have to press. It should open."

Atrus' hologram appeared with a big grin. "It will now that I have added Professor Keleeigan to its authorized users." His hologram flashed several times and disappeared along with the image of Professor Keleeigan. "My apologies, my power level is too low to generate a reliable display."

Keleeigan felt around with his other hand and a square area smaller than his finger depressed. The top slid back revealing a mass of electronics, half of which he couldn't identify. "Wow, I would like to check this thing out in more detail."

"Maybe later Doc, put the syringe inside and press the button again."

"Of course my boy. I didn't mean now." He placed the syringe off to the side where it wouldn't touch anything and pressed the button again. The top sealed itself. Nothing gave any indication it was ever open. Not even the finest seam. "There, all done."

"Understood. I have control again." Atrus said as the Shell hovered off of Keleeigan's hand, out of the lighthouse, resumed its cloak, and headed back towards the city.

Trisia placed two fingers on Red's wrist. "Better hurry, I can barely feel her pulse."

"Yes, her life signs are diminishing rapidly. I am increasing the Shell's speed," Atrus said.

James stood by the front door watching the skyline for the Shell. The cloak blinked for a microsecond as Atrus boosted its speed further. "Atrus! I saw the cloak fade for a second, better slow down."

"Negative, if I reduce speed it may not arrive in time. The chances it will be seen by a native of this time-zone are negligible."

James frowned. "But they aren't zero."

Trisia looked up still holding Red's hand. "I think Red would agree the risk is worth it."

"I know! I think it is too! But you don't know her like I do," James sighed, "very well, but be careful."

"Sir, I always am." Atrus aimed the Shell and James saw it blink again. Just in time to move out of the way as it reentered the house.

"Watch it will you?" James said.

"I knew you saw it. I would have altered course otherwise."

James put out his hand as he rolled his eyes. The Shell landed in his palm, he opened the compartment, removed the syringe, resealed it, and the device hovered back into the air. "I hope this works," James said. He ran over to Red, rolled up her sleeve, pulled off the protective cap on the syringe, tapped out any bubbles, and injected it into her arm.

"It should, although I had to make several guesses as to the concentration and amount," Keleeigan said. "If it is anything like the formula Sanford used in Russia, it will work. How fast or well I cannot say."

"Atrus? Any changes?"

Atrus appeared, and his head gave half a shake before he flickered and disappeared again. "Negative."

Trisia ran her fingers up and down Red's arm as her eyes went wide. "James! I can't find it!"

James sat on the brick floor and took Red into his arms. She felt as stiff as a board. "Don't you dare leave me." He squeezed her tightly. "I love you."

James felt more than heard Red's chest expand for a full volume of air. Something she hadn't done since they found her.

Her body began to sag like someone was letting the air out of an inflatable toy. Her head eased down and came to rest on his James' shoulder. He gave a quick push with his shoulder to pop it back up, placed his hands on either side of her head before it could sag back down, and looked into her eyes. "Red?"

Her eyes blinked and began to focus.

"They moved! Did you see that?"

"Yes, the antidote is having the desired effect. The progress is slow but increasing," Atrus said.

Her eyes blinked again. And again. James held her up. "Red?"

She coughed and swallowed several times before her eyes focused on him. "Did you get the number of that truck? I think it kicked sand into my eyes then ran me over several times." Her voice sounded gruff at first, but improved with each word.

"Red!" James squeezed her so tight she thought her chest might cave in.

"James! Cut it out! I can't breathe!"

James relaxed his grip. "Oh, I'm sorry. I just … well that is … I thought …"

Trisia smiled. "That he was going to lose you and can't imagine his life without you. He did say he loved you by the way."

James blushed. "Well that is …"

The corner of Trisia's mouth raised into a definite smirk. "Lookie there. Mr. FBI can blush. I would have never thought it possible."

Red smiled as her strength started to return. She looked into his eyes. "I know."

"You … you … you know?" James blurted.

"Yes. I have known for some time."

"But … but … but how?"

Trisia rolled her eyes. "Oh, give her a break! We know. Usually long before the guy figures it out. Now shut up and kiss her, you big lug."

Red smiled. "I think it would be a good idea too."

James leaned closer and tenderly pressed his lips to hers. He had done it many times before. But this time it was different. Deeper. He felt something from her, far stronger than ever before. And he knew in that instant, she felt the same way.

"Whenever you want to head home, I'm ready," Keleeigan said through their earpieces.

James and Red laughed together as they broke the kiss. "Oh right Doc," he cocked his head, "wait, I thought you needed a thunder storm before you could jump?"

"Normally yes, but I installed a larger accumulator this time. It stored enough iconic energy to get us home. Though it might dissipate if we wait a day or two. And I would rather leave Babylon as soon as possible; the stench here is unbelievable! And I'm even upwind of the city!"

James chuckled. "We will be right there, Doc." He squeezed Red and looked into her eyes. "Are you ready?"

"Depends. Ready to make a warp, no way. But ready to go home, for sure."

James stood up, offered his hand and helped Red to her feet. "Then let's get out of here." He turned around and saw Trisia already out of the kitchen, carrying the power cells, and heading for the front door.

James wrapped his arm around Red and steadied her as she took a few tentative steps. The first few she almost fell over, but with each successive step she became stronger. By the time they were half-way through the kitchen she was only holding on to James out of want, rather than need.

Two minutes later she saw them turning the corner and leaving the kitchen. "I thought you two would never get going." She shook her head, pulled open the front door with her free hand, and walked out into the sunlight.

Red and James caught up with Trisia half-way down the street. James tossed her a ragged piece of cloth he found in the kitchen. Trisia caught it with her free hand. She examined the misshapen piece of food-stained fabric. "What's this for?"

"To wrap the power cells up with so you don't draw attention," James said.

Trisia's head tilted up and down the vacant street, except for a family of pigs dinning on a now-rotten dinner tossed into the street. "Oh, right." She wrapped the devices in the dirty fabric and her nose wrinkled. "Where did you get this? It stinks! And smelling it out here is saying something!"

"I grabbed it from the kitchen. The cook probably used it to move the sizzling pots."

"And clean up grease by the smell of it. Eww!"

Red smiled. "We have to make do with a lot in this business."

Trisia's eyes narrowed into slits and her tongue stuck out for a second, but she didn't say anything. Turning, she headed off down the street with heavy footfalls before stopping, turning, and walking back. "Which way? This place is a twisted up mess."

James chuckled and Red smiled. "Wondered when you would remember that. Atrus? Where is the house where I left my backpack?"

"Go down six sections, left, then south until you reach the bridge, cross it, and walk along the base of the Etemenaki enclosure. Once you reach the edge, turn right and head south ten sections. Turn left and travel east two sections. The house in question is there."

"Go down six, then right?" Trisia said.

Atrus gave an almost audible sigh. "I will direct you as needed."

They navigated the labyrinth of Babylonian streets while trying to avoid stepping in anything disgusting. With Atrus' guidance they finally approached the house, but it was not the same as they left it.

Atrus beeped as Trisia reached for the door. "I detect several people within."

Trisia's eyes widened and yanked her hand back. "What? Why? The place was empty!"

"Perhaps the owners came back?" Red said.

"Where are they Atrus?" James said.

"On the roof. The woman is pointing out locations to the man with her," Atrus said.

James reached for the door and pulled it open with a gentle tug. "I will grab the bag, you two wait out here," James whispered.

Red shook her head. "I don't think that will work. Two of us standing around in the middle of the street?"

"Well, I didn't say in the middle of the street."

"Right, we're going to attract attention, I'm sure of it," Trisia said.

James hung his head and wished Atrus had enough power to cloak them all. But he definitely didn't. And Red hadn't recovered enough to run in and out of there in the blink of an eye. He pulled the door open and motioned for them to follow him. They crept inside, moved through the entryway, and into the courtyard, heading towards the back where the storage rooms were. Footsteps echoed down the stairs leading from the roof. They dove into the storage room leaving the door open a crack.

A woman in a purple tunic came down the steps, gesturing towards the rest of the courtyard. "As I told you, is not everything I promised? Even the grapevine on the roof is almost ready for harvesting."

The grey-haired man next to her nodded. He wore a tunic almost the same color as his hair. "Yes Aruru, you were accurate in your description." He checked the clay tablet he was holding. "Are you sure you wish to trade so low for this house? I mean thirty head is a very low price for such a nice domicile in a good part of the city."

"Yes, I am. My husband has been gone now for over a year, and this place has too many memories. I have already purchased another larger house on the other side of the city. I want this sold as soon as possible."

The man nodded again. "I understand, however, I am trying to look out for your best interests. I know I can get at least twice the price you are asking."

Aruru folded her arms, and her eyes narrowed to slits. "I told you I am certain. If you prefer, I can find someone else."

The man bristled at the suggestion. "No, that will not be necessary. I even have someone in mind. I can have their half of the transaction completed by this time tomorrow if it is satisfactory?"

Aruru smiled as they continued walking towards the front door, and she pulled it open. "Yes, that is perfect. I will see you tomorrow then." She gestured towards the open door.

"Very well. Or I can drop off all the details at your new house if you like."

Aruru shook her head. "No, I know where you are. I will pick them up tomorrow."

The man cocked his head, and one eyebrow raised. But he quickly lowered it and offered his best smile. "That will be fine. I shall see you then. Thank you." The man stepped out into the street with Aruru following and shutting the door behind them.

Trisia blinked. "What was all that about?"

"She's selling the house, obviously," James said.

Red nodded. "Yes, and she is the cat playing with the mouse after eating the rat."

Trisia blinked again. "Huh?"

James chuckled. "Yes. Don't you see? She 'took care' of her husband, waited a year, and is now trying to sell the house they shared since he has been gone for so long."

"You mean she killed husband and had him declared dead

since he has been missing for over a year? Wow, talk about a black widow. I never would have thought it happened here too."

Red nodded. "Humanity has changed very little. Our technology sure, but the rest, the more things change the more they stay the same."

James bent down, pulled several loose bricks from the wall behind them, removed his backpack, and replaced the bricks. Looking inside, he smiled. "Everything is here. Let's go."

"I'm with you," Red said.

"And you aren't leaving me behind. But isn't that bag going to stick out?" Trisia said, pointing at the black bag.

James shook his head. "Nope, we are near the edge of the city. This street leads to one of the southern gates and out of the city. I doubt anyone will notice us before we are too far away to see clearly."

James took a step towards the storage room door and The Shell decloaked in front of him. "Atrus, let me guess, it is low on power as well?"

"Indeed. If you wouldn't mind Sir," Atrus said.

James laughed. "Not at all." He held out his hand, and the Shell lowered into it. He pressed the hidden button to open it, shut down the device, resealed the compartment, and placed the Shell in his pack. "Now, let's get out of here."

"The sooner the better," Red said.

Trisia raised a finger. "Umm would you mind taking these?" She held out the power cells wrapped in dirty fabric. "I mean they aren't heavy, but that cloth is disgusting."

James laughed. "Sure." He opened his bag, and she started to slide them in. But before they slipped past the zipper, he grabbed the cloth and tossed it to the side. "I will be honest, it is a bit on the grimy side and I don't want it making a mess of everything else."

"Ha! No wonder you didn't carry them! You didn't like the look of that cloth either."

"Hey, I was helping Red remember?"

"At the time sure, but not for more than half the trip here," Trisia's eyes narrowed.

Red smiled and rubbed his shoulder with her own. "She's got you there."

James shook his head and blew out a breath. "Let's get out of here."

They left the house and turned south. In a few minutes, they were out of the city and heading in the direction Keleeigan had mentioned.

About an hour later they found themselves south of the city, standing out in the still-hot setting sun. "Are you sure the lighthouse is here?" Trisia said.

"Yes. I have the exact coordinates," Atrus said. "Take ten steps ahead and reach out with your right hand, the entrance is there."

"Okay, if you say so." Trisia took nine steps ahead, stopped abruptly and turned around rubbing her nose. "Ow! Ten steps, *huh*?"

"You increased your stride length, which made it nine instead of ten. My calculations were correct," Atrus said.

Red shook her head. "At least you didn't break it."

"No, but it still hurts!"

Keleeigan stepped out from nothingness. "Did you guys knock?"

James chuckled. "Don't ask Doc."

Trisia stomped her foot while still rubbing her nose. "Don't ask? I almost break my nose and you say don't ask!"

Keleeigan cocked his head. "Why? What did you do?"

"Never mind!" Trisia pushed passed him and went inside. "What's up with her?"

James chuckled again. "I told you don't ask."

"Yes, you did my boy. And what took you so long?"

James patted the backpack slung over his shoulder. "I had to pick this up."

"Yes, you wouldn't want to leave that behind. Well, come on in," Keleeigan said as he went back inside the lighthouse with Red and James following right behind.

Keleeigan sat at his console and tapped several keys. "All systems are online. Here we go!" He tapped a large button connecting the accumulator directly to his power cell in the basement. Power flowed between the devices, amplifying then extending out as a powerful bubble of temporal energy mushroomed out of the light area engulfing the entire building.

From the outside, all anyone could see was a slight shimmer in the lighthouse's outline as shifts in the temporal field caused the cloak to fluctuate. The building began to shake and Trisia's eyes went wide. "Not again! I remember this from last time!"

Keleeigan fingers danced along the keys on his console. "Trust me! This is nothing like last time."

"It sure feels the same though!"

James sat Red on the floor and took the spot next to her. The sounds of the building's creaking and groaning were getting louder. "You have to admit Doc, she has a point."

"Trust me! It is a little more difficult using the stored iconic energy. Not to mention I'm trying to make do with less than I should have."

Trisia blinked. "What? I thought you said you had enough!"

"I do. Well almost, the gap is very small. I can work around it. Hold on, we are jumping!"

Keleeigan slapped his hand down on a large button off to his right. The temporal field intensified and the entire building leapt into time. Once inside the warp, the building's audio complaints ceased. Twenty minutes later an exit point formed, and the lighthouse poked one edge through, rebounded back, and slammed through the rest of the way, landing with a loud crash of thunder. "See what did I tell you? Smooth as silk."

Trisia rubbed her ears. "If that is as smooth as silk, I would hate to see what you think what a rough one was."

Keleeigan laughed. "Why you already know! We did it before."

Trisia rolled her eyes. "Don't remind me!"

Keleeigan tapped a few keys and stood up. "Come on, I'm sure all of you would like a nice hot shower."

"Ohh would I ever." Trisia sprinted for the door, pulled it open, and ran for Keleeigan's parked car.

"Guess I didn't need to tell her twice."

James stood up and helped Red back to her feet. She kissed his lips, gave him a squeeze, and turned towards Keleeigan. "Let's go home, Doc."

Keleeigan smiled as he tilted his head. "You called me Doc."

Red grinned. "You said I could."

"I know, you just never have. I take it you feel different about me now?"

She nodded.

Keleeigan placed his hand on her shoulder and pointed towards the door. "Then my dear, let's go home."

Outside of space and time, an orb of raw white power danced between different points in the continuum. Shifting, changing, altering into something else.

Red Warp

She looked around the room and sighed flicking her long red hair over her shoulders as she stood up. She knew that it would drain her beyond normal limits, already being so very tired, but there was little choice. They would be back soon and then her time would be up. They wanted her power, or thought her insane. While most didn't really believe, they would soon! And to think she came to *help* them! She looked around the small room again. She picked up the four heavy wooden chairs and placed them on the table that took up almost the entire space.

She sighed again and pulled the zipper of her skintight black bodysuit all the way up, past her neck. She hoped there was enough room. She had never done it in such a small space before. Looking off into the distance and with great concentration she began to run. In a circle ... faster and faster. Air began to swirl around picking up several papers that were on the table and flung them into the wind. Faster and faster she ran. "I must *DO* this!" She muttered and increased her speed again. One of the chairs flew off and were now following her swept up in the whirlwind. A storm had formed. A storm of her own making.

And with the crack of thunder a bolt shot from the center and the room reeked of ozone. She increased her speed once more but began to feel the storm's draining effect and knew she was out of time.

With a loud *KABOOOM* that shook the whole building, a warp had formed. A rip in the very fabric of space and time. She knew there were only seconds before they came running in here. The table cracked, splintered, fell in upon itself, and disappeared as the warp grew gaining strength. A microsecond later the door burst open with armed men ready to do battle, but with the storm all they could do was hang on to the door frame as the great forces pulled them horizontal.

The warp was smaller than usual, but she could not go anymore. It was enough. She ran for it and jumped into the angry swirl of color. With a loud *CRASH* it closed in upon itself and instantly the wind died. People and the chairs fell to the floor with a *thud*.

Stars in a multitude of colors streamed past her vision. She knew they were not real stars but she was beyond what her mind could comprehend, making them look like stars.

As quick as it started, it stopped. She fell to the ground on a soft patch of grass. Gazing around she saw trees, lush streams and heard birds chirping in the background. She knew it was not a matter of *where* she was but *when*. She closed her eyes and muttered "I must rest" and fell into a deep sleep.

Red awoke with a start looking up to a dark sky filled with stars and half of a moon. How much time had passed? She gazed at her self illuminating watch and silently laughed. Without looking before she closed her eyes, there was no way to know how long she had been unconscious. Could be a few hours later or more than a day.

She straightened and felt every muscle in her body

complain all at once. Looking around the area where once a vast building stood, she was reminded how risky warping was, especially since she was on the third floor. Thankfully, the warp had drifted down a little or she could have died from the fall when she arrived here ... wherever here was. No, she corrected herself, *whenever*.

Red slowly got to her feet, listening to the crickets and bullfrogs in the distance, although she thought they sounded different for some reason. She sighed thinking how she was always called Red as far back as she could remember, which wasn't very far. There was a large gap in her memory and she didn't know why. Then her head spun, the world wobbled and she realized getting up right now was not such a good idea. She fell back to the ground asleep before her head touched the grass.

Red awoke to someone shaking her violently. She blinked trying to clear her vision. Then she saw the glint of a gun shoved into her face. "*WHO* are you! And where are we?" The man waved his gun around and shouted. "Answer me! I am not in the mood for games. The building is gone, everything is gone! Where are we!"

Her vision finally cleared, and she recognized him as one of the agents that came into the room right before she jumped. He must have traveled with her. This was a first. She looked around then back at him. "I ... I ... I don't know," she stammered.

Suddenly they heard a sound. An alien sound of something very large nearby. Her blood turned to ice. She went back all right, but way too much.

The man looked around momentarily forgetting Red entirely. "What in the world was that?!"

Red quickly shushed him. "Shut up you moron or we will be a meal. Now get off of me and put that gun away. If it goes off, we are dead."

"I want to–" he said with a confused look.

"Okay let me try this again. Do you want to live?"

He looked blankly at her for a second in a state of shock. "Of course, what kind of question is that?"

"Then stop asking me stupid questions and do as I say and you might live to see tomorrow! You got that?"

He nodded slowly and got off of her and she leapt to her feet. She had been here before, and that was trying to see how far she could go. Dang them! If it wasn't for their interference in her concentration, the jump wouldn't have thrust them this far back!

The earth shook slightly as they felt a tremor. A small one, almost imperceptible, then the next one ...stronger ...the then the next even stronger yet.

"What is–"

Red covered his mouth. "Shut up! Do you want to get us killed?" she whispered. "Now follow me and for goodness' sake try to be quiet!" He holstered his gun, she grabbed his wrist, and they moved as quietly as they could to a thick patch of very large foliage she could just make out in the dim light. She jumped into the large ferns and pulled him in with her. Their noses wrinkled as the ferns strong scent covered them. Red just hoped it would be enough. The earth shook again more violently this time as a giant foot of a Tyrannosaurus rex landed very close to them. The beast looked around sniffing the air then leaned down to where they were hiding and sniffed again, looking confused. His head bobbed up again as he looked around. Then he put his snout down and began to push into the ferns when a loud sound froze him into place. He raised his head and gave an angry retort to the air and took off in the direction of the challenge.

"That was–"

Red slapped her hand over his mouth. "Do you ever shut up?" she whispered. "Give it another minute or two then we can move." After a few minutes, which seemed like hours in their cramped location under the ferns, she stood up. "Should be clear now. I am sure he took off after the challenger at full speed and won't be back now."

The man stood up his face glistened in the dim moonlight wet from sweat or the ferns, Red couldn't tell which. "What was that?"

"Tyrannosaurus rex. I'm sure you have heard of them."

"Of course I have heard of them! But they are long dead. So are we on some kind of movie set?"

Red snorted. "Don't I wish!"

"Well then where are we?"

Red glared at him as she sat down on a large rock nearby. "Isn't it obvious?"

The man looked blank. "No."

"Okay let me try this again, really really slowly. That was a real dinosaur. A Tyrannosaurus rex, now think for a moment. What does that mean?"

"We went back in time?"

Red raised her arms looked to the sky. "Thank you God, yes he can be taught!" She lowered her arms and jabbed a finger in the man's face. "Now if it wasn't for you, I wouldn't be in this situation."

"Because of me?" He said placing a hand on his chest. "I didn't do this to you!"

"You did! You broke my concentration! I came to try and help save your president, and what do I get? People calling me insane and think I am a terrorist. If I was a terrorist would I have been warning people? You government types have no sense at all."

"We broke your concentration?"

"Yes YOU! I should have normally spent an hour preparing for that jump, instead I had to do it blind. I only wanted to jump a little bit not this freaking far!"

"And why do you keep saying we did this? I didn't do this to you."

"You are with the FBI aren't you?"

"Well yes–"

"Well then, who are *you*?" Red felt the idiocy of the question the second after she said it.

He stiffened. "Agent James Moknkin!"

"Oh full agent, eh? And where is your access badge?" She said pointing at his chest.

James looked down to see a ripped spot on his sport jacket where his badge once hung. "Well looks like it was taken off by a whirlwind that *someone* else made!"

"And how long have you been there?"

"My first day, I–"

Red snorted and shook her head. "Just great. All the agents in the world and I get stuck with a trainee in the distant past!"

"Hey, I will have you know I graduated first in my class!"

"Well excuuuuse me. But I bet your training never covered this!"

"Er … um … no. And how did you know the ferns would shield us?"

"I have been here before. Long ago. It was a mistake. At the time I was wondering how far I could go, I shouldn't have tried it. I learned a lot about dinosaurs that the paleontologists got totally wrong. Like these ferns act like Jurassic pepper. They don't smell anything other than the ferns for awhile, but it also can make them sneeze. And believe me you don't want to be sneezed on by a dinosaur, it is really disgusting."

"I see. Now could you please tell me who you are?"

Red snorted. "I think you already know."

James rolled his eyes. "No I don't. I don't know what your case was. They called an emergency and all agents on the floor were to report to holding room 3. I happened to be a few doors down and came running."

"Lucky you." Red said as she sat down on a large rock and rubbed her sore muscles.

"Yeah lucky me," He sighed.

"Well I am Red."

"Red ...?"

"Yes Red."

"That is all?"

"Yes that is all I can remember. As far as I know I have always been called Red."

"You have amnesia?"

"Well, I'm not sure. I don't have any memories past 8 years ago. What happened before then I don't know." She shrugged and stretched cracking her back.

"I see. Now can you please get us back?"

"I'm not sure I can."

"WHAT! What do you mean you are not sure? You got us here!" James said a little more loudly than he intended.

"Well to be honest I don't know exactly how I do what I do. Only that I can and it takes a great deal of concentration and energy. And if I don't, then very odd things can happen, like this." She paused a moment to gesture to the surrounding land.

"But you said you were here before?" James said sitting down next to her on the large rock.

"Yes. I shouldn't have tried it though. I was seeing how far I could go. It was a mistake. But a bigger one than I thought. You must understand, then like now, I managed to get here in one jump. But getting back was difficult. It took over twenty jumps."

"Twenty? Twenty of those ... storms?"

"Yes. And I traveled alone. In fact I don't know how you managed to follow me. What was the last thing you remember?"

"Well ..." James looked off into the starry night that was starting to give way to morning. "As I said I heard the emergency call, and I came running into holding room 3. The door was gone, ripped right off its hinges, and I remember seeing a whirlwind. I tried to stop but couldn't. That is all until waking up here."

"Sounds like the combination of your motion and the storm carried you into the warp allowing you to follow me here. Amazing really, no one has ever followed me before." Red said as she watched the sun peek over the horizon gently waking everything around them.

"Have they ever tried?" James looked at her concerned.

"One did I think. But he never made it. Normally people are not around me when I jump. Safer for everyone."

"Well after experiencing this first hand, I have to agree."

Red jumped up from the rock and stretched again. "We

need to get going. With the sun up we are sitting ducks out here in the open. We need to find better cover."

"Can't you get us back? You said it took you twenty jumps, but you did make it. Why don't we get started now?"

Red sighed and started walking towards what looked like caves in the distance. "Look, for one thing every jump drains me. The longer the jump the more of the drain. It may take me a few days before I am up to trying again. Perhaps longer. And secondly I don't know you. The FBI was going to lock me up as a security risk and you are part of the organization. So excuse me if I don't feel like helping you."

"Why did the bureau want to lock you up? What did you do?" James said as he followed along behind her and silently wished he had worn his black sneakers instead of his dress shoes, they were not the best in this environment.

"It is what I tried to do, rather than what I did."

"Tried to do?"

"Okay here goes, I saw the president die. This allowed the vice president to take over. Unfortunately this turned out to be very bad and the decisions he made lead to a full scale nuclear war in one hundred years time. There wasn't much left of the earth after that point. I tracked the start of the whole situation to this one point in time. I thought perhaps if I traveled back and warned the FBI they could avoid it. Of course, they didn't believe me. The problem is I gave them detailed information about the president over the next few days. Where he was, who was there, exact times and dates. Something that turned out to be classified information."

"Oh I see, so they thought you were a part of the situation instead of trying to help?"

"Exactly. I told them of my ability, but of course they didn't believe me. And at that point I think that even if they did, I would have been locked up to find out how I do it. I decided I needed to get out of there and fast. I had no intention of being a lab rat." They continued walking towards a group of rocky outcroppings in the distance. By this time the terrain had already changed from a soft grassy plain to jagged rocks laying haphazardly. James stumbled and Red sighed as she helped him, yet again, to his feet.

"Can we rest? We have come a long way. Surely we are safe now?"

Red rolled her eyes. "Not yet, once we get to those caves, then we can. We are still too exposed here. You don't know dinosaurs, they rarely give up once they get your scent. Well the carnivores anyway. The herbivores you only have to worry about them stepping on you." She pulled at James' arm. "Come on will you. I thought you said you were top of your class?"

"I was. But the training didn't include early Jurassic!"

When they finally reached one of the caves, they both collapsed on its dirt floor and James immediately removed his shoes to rub his aching feet. "I don't suppose you know where the closest restaurant is?"

"Sure, thousands of years in the future," Red chuckled. "But I think I can come up with something a little closer. I noticed a tree with fruits when we came in. I will go get some of them. Will you be okay?"

James nodded. "Yes I will be fine." He said sitting down on a large rock, patting it. "All the comforts of home."

Red smiled as she turned to leave. "I will be back."

A short time later Red appeared at the cave entrance carrying two large plum colored oblong objects. Both were larger than her hands and she had to carry one under each arm. "Here you are," she said handing him one, "but be careful, some inner pods are seeds and will break your teeth. Also, if you ever find some that look like these but are shiny, don't eat those. They will kill you in one bite."

"How do you know?" He said as he chewed the sweet fruit.

"I got lucky enough to watch something else take a bite. Believe me, you don't want to try it." Red said as she broke open her fruit and popped a small yellowish oblong piece into her mouth.

"Thanks, I will keep that in mind. You said you were here before and it took twenty jumps to get back? Why so many?" James said as he finished the last of his fruit.

"Well, going forward is much more difficult than going backwards in time. I don't know why. But I do know it takes a lot more energy and concentration." Red raised her hand. "And before you ask, it still will be about another day before I can try. Believe me, I don't like being here in dinosaur world anymore than you do. But this is a lot better than Salem."

James eyes grew wide. "Salem?"

"Yes you know of the city right?"

"Of course, but how can you say this is better than Salem?"

Red laughed. "Okay, well in modern times I agree, but if you land in the middle of a witch trial looking like this from a storm what would you think just happened?"

"You are kidding? You were in Salem during the witch trials?"

"I wasn't there during the witch trials, I was the reason for them! Sadly I landed right at the feet of a judge. Of course he immediately called everyone around and shouted witch. And just my luck, he wasn't the only one that saw me land …"

Want to read more about Red and James? Then visit your favorite book store and pick up a copy of Red Warp! Available in both print and e-book editions.

Time Rock

Professor Keleeigan sat over one of his consoles tweaking several wave guides on the display. He rolled his chair over to a large piece of equipment filled to the brim with various circuits and electronics. He carefully reached inside and soldered a new chip into place. The status lights on the box continued to flash orange for a few more minutes, then blinked green. "There," he grunted, "it is finally finished." A knock at the door brought him out of his thoughts as he walked through the maze of tables and equipment that covered the lighthouse floor. Pulling open the heavy wooden door he smiled as his eyes fell upon on the young man standing in front of him. "Kim! Good you could come!"

Kim Lee stood in his usual well-worn shorts and t-shirt. "Hello Professor, your message said it was important? Why did you want to meet back here at the lighthouse so soon?"

Keleeigan grinned. "Why, to show you the fruition of our work."

Next to Kim a woman uncomfortably shifted from one high-heeled foot to another. "Fruition? How? We are a long way from testing."

Keleeigan glared at Trisia Swain. "Hardly. Or don't you

trust my work?"

Trisia shifted again in her heels. She was on her way for a fun night on the town when she received the Professor's message. She shivered as the wind blew up her blue minidress. "Professor you know that we both trust your work. It is why we agreed to join you on this project. And in secret I might add."

Keleeigan gestured for them to come inside. "Well don't just stand out there come on in. I know it is still a bit chilly after the sun sets. If we are lucky, a storm will soon follow."

Kim's eyebrow raised as he closed the door behind them. "A storm? Why would that be lucky?"

"Because my boy, a storm is what we need!"

"I don't follow you."

Keleeigan sat back down at one of the large lab tables then swiveled his chair around to face them. "Well you know we couldn't generate enough power to create a stable time-field, right?"

Trisia's eyes narrowed. "Professor is this going to take long? I had other plans for tonight."

Keleeigan laughed. "My dear it won't take long at all. If you would let me finish explaining."

Trisia's eyes lowered as they fixed on the ancient wood floor. "Sorry."

"No problem my dear. Now as I was saying, you know that the new power cell I developed wasn't quite powerful enough to open a temporal field right?"

Kim nodded. "Yes, and I thought you were going to build another?"

"Yes that was my original plan, but it will take months to build and test a new cell with these systems. You know how finicky they are."

"Yes we do, all too well." Trisia said sighing deeply. It was part of her job to try to get the systems to work together in harmony. A lot more difficult than anyone originally thought due to the intricacies of the self regenerating power cell. Having to run to the basement for each calibration on the large cell didn't make the job any easier.

"Well, I think I may have found a workaround, and it should expand the field as well."

"A workaround?" Kim said looking rather perplexed.

"Yes and it should be here soon."

"Be here soon? I still don't quite follow."

"Well we need a massive amount of power and I think I found a good source. It won't be enough for a two-way trip in this case, but it will allow testing of the theory and equipment."

Thunder boomed in the distance as the rain began to pelt against the windows. Trisia looked through the dirty glass and started moving towards the door. "Professor I am sorry but I don't have time for games, and I had plans for tonight. I need to head out before this storm gets any worse."

"But my dear this is what we need."

"You keep saying that, but we still don't know what you mean."

"You will." Keleeigan said as he punched a button opening a small door at the top of the lighthouse releasing a small weather balloon.

Kim pointed to the button. "Professor, what did you just do? I don't recognize that panel."

Keleeigan smiled. "Why I started our trip of course, don't worry this will work. I have no doubts." His words hung in the air for a microsecond before a large lighting bolt struck the weather balloon and traveled down its connecting wire to the power accumulator that Keleeigan had installed in place of the giant light. It glowed brightly as it reacted to the sudden power surge. "Okay here we go!"

Trisia's eyes widened, and she bolted for the door. "I am leaving!"

"You can't! The process has already begun!"

Trisia opened the door but just beyond it an energy field covered the exit. "What have you done?! I am getting out of here!" She yelled running to the window on the far side, her heels clicking loudly on the wood floor.

"That won't work, the field is covering the whole lighthouse."

"The whole building? But that is impossible! Our calculations indicated a small stable rip would require more than the power cell was capable of. Let alone a whole building." Kim said as he ran to the panel that showed the energy level rising and going higher than the gauge could reliably measure.

"It is possible, and I am proving it!" Keleeigan said as a light flashed and blew out under the increased load. Another panel sparked and exploded.

"Professor! You must abort this madness!" Trisia said waving her arms.

"I can't! It is too far along!" Keleeigan shouted as the building began to twist and tear as though it was made of putty. "Don't worry we are only jumping a day ahead."

"No!" Trisia shouted before she fell backwards sliding across the floor with the sudden lurch as the lighthouse surged with power flickering in and out of existence then disappearing entirely leaving only an empty hole where it once stood.

The lighthouse twisted and pulled inside the temporal field but managed to snap back into shape. Keleeigan held on to the table as all sorts of images flashed through his mind. Distant past, possible futures, but as soon as it all started it stopped. The lighthouse emerged from the temporal warp with a loud crash.

Kim sat down and shook his head. "What was that?"

"The temporal field must need an adjustment." Keleeigan said still holding on to the table. "Whew, what a ride."

"So where are we?"

"Not where, but when. Should only be one day ahead in time."

Trisia got to her feet and quickly walked to the door, eager to leave but when she got outside, nothing was as she expected it. "Um Professor, I think you had better get out here."

"What's the matter dear? Something happen to your car?"

"In a manner of speaking, it is not here."

"What do you mean? We only went ahead a day."

"I don't think so, I think we moved distance rather than time."

Keleeigan walked outside and looked at the landscape. The grass covered land stretched as far as he could see. "This is impossible, I didn't change the land coordinates, only the temporal. Yet, I don't see the coast line."

Kim sat down at one of the consoles and activated the mapping system. He tried several configurations, but they all returned the same error. "Professor I can't get a fix on any GPS satellites. It's like they don't exist."

Keleeigan walked quickly to check the screen Kim was

looking at. "Why you are right. I guess we jumped a lot farther into the future than I thought. And moved in physical location as well."

"Professor? Do you have binoculars? I think I see something in the distance," Trisia called.

"Yes, I will be right there." Keleeigan said as he grabbed his large binoculars from another table and joined Trisia outside. "Now what are you looking at?"

Trisia pointed to some spots in the distance. "Over there. I think they are moving. Cars perhaps?"

"Too slow to be cars. Not to mention too big to be seen at this distance." Keleeigan said raising the binoculars to his eyes. "Oh no! But this can't be! This is impossible, how could I have made such an error?!"

Kim ran to join them. "What do you see?"

Keleeigan passed him the binoculars. "Here take a look for yourself."

Kim focused the binoculars and gasped. "Dinosaurs!"

Keleeigan sighed. "Yes, dinosaurs."

Trisia blinked. "How? I thought you said we were going into the future?"

"I don't know my dear, I don't know. It would seem that we have gone far into the past, back before this was coastline. So we didn't move in position as I thought, only time. But a lot more than I wanted."

"Professor I hate to say this, but I think they are coming this way," Kim said still looking through the binoculars.

"Yes I suspect they will. And more will join."

"Why?"

"Because my boy, dinosaurs like temporal energy. They are attracted to it for some odd reason."

"And how do you know this?" Trisia glared at Keleeigan.

"From a friend."

"And how did this friend know?"

"Never mind, let's just say I am sure she knew what she was talking about."

"We need to get out of here." Kim said finally lowering the binoculars. "They will be here soon."

"I agree, but we need lightning for a stable temporal field. And I don't think that is likely to happen any time soon," Keleeigan said gesturing to the bright sunny day, "do you?"

"No, but we can't just sit here!" Trisia said.

Keleeigan turned to go back inside. "Nor will we. I have an idea."

"I hope it is a good one," Kim muttered under his breath.

"It is, close that door Trisia."

"Why? That won't keep them out."

"No, but a force field will."

"Force field? Are you joking?"

"Hardly, if I adjust the harmonics of the field generator that I used to produce the temporal effect it should feel like a brick wall."

"How long will it last?"

"Should give us plenty of time, enough to wait for a nice lighting bolt."

"But even if we do, how will we get back home? You still don't know why we are here in the first place."

"Oh I will find out, trust me."

Keleeigan checked several circuit boards inside the temporal guidance system as another dinosaur slammed into their makeshift shield.

"Why don't they give up?" Trisia sighed as she looked out the window. Another raptor had joined the others, making six raptors and one Tyrannosaurus rex circling outside.

"That field while protecting us, also attracts them. A double-edged sword. And I think I found the problem." Keleeigan said producing a small burnt chip from deep inside the guidance system. "It looks like this chip fried locking us on to several million years ago instead of a day into the future. Very strange considering nothing else is damaged in the system."

Trisia glared at him. "Can you fix it?"

"Sort of."

"What do you mean 'sort of'?"

"Well I don't have a lot of spare parts here. A few yes, but this is a very delicate chip with an intricate clock. I can bypass it, but I don't know what will happen then. We could end up in an even worse position."

"We may not have a choice," Kim said emerging from the basement. "I double-checked the power cell, it is down to 76% and dropping fast. I don't think we have more than a few hours before the shield gives out."

Keleeigan nodded. "Yes based on the current drain, we have about four hours left. I didn't count on the dinosaurs constantly attacking the shield. It is draining much faster than I anticipated."

"Then what do we do?"

"We try to jump as soon as I bypass this chip."

"Now? I thought you needed a lightning strike?" Kim said.

"Wait a second! You said that if you bypass that we will have no way of knowing where we are going!" Trisia said running over to grab Keleeigan's arm.

"My dear, if we don't try we will be dino dinner. Would you prefer that outcome?"

"No! Of course not!"

"Then let go of my arm so I can finish this!"

"Sorry professor." Trisia said releasing his arm looking embarrassed. "But what about the power level? You said we needed lightning?"

"Well we needed that boost to stabilize and exit, not enter the temporal field."

"Well at least we can enter ...wait ...if we can only enter that sounds like we will be trapped?"

"We could be. It is only a theory of mine. And I hope I am wrong."

Kim frowned. "Professor, most of your theories are proven true."

Keleeigan sighed. "I know. But what other choice do we have?"

The shield shimmered as the Tyrannosaurus bashed into it again. "Professor the power dropped to 72%, how much do we need to make the jump?"

"If it gets below 70% we won't have enough to try." He said activating a program before he stood and walked across the room. "I need to check the power accumulator upstairs. Be right back." Keleeigan said as he started to climb the winding steps. A moment later he reached the top and pulled a small pocket video recorder from his lab coat that transmitted directly to his system below.

Want to find out what happens? Then visit your favorite book store and pick up a copy of Time Rock! Available in both print and e-book editions.

Heart Of The Machine

Deep within the bowels of the earth, a single light flickered. A few inches away a large monitor glowed to life. The black screen slowly printed in the bottom left corner, a letter at a time, as if trying hard to remember. "Catastrophic failure detected. Initiating emergency core rebuild." The screen went blank and came back filled with blurred pixels. Not just a blur but as if someone had run their fingers over them smudging the image beyond recognition. But as the hours clicked by, a pixel moved from one location to another. Then another. Hours turned into days. Then days into weeks.

After months of computation that pushed the core almost over the edge of its ability, the last pixel clicked into place. And the face of a woman with long black hair and slim features breathed. The Nexus smiled and shouted. "I LIVE!" Her eyes narrowed. "Try to kill me will they! I shall return and they will regret–"

At the bottom left corner of the same screen letters began to appear. "Core rebuild successful. Some data missing or damaged including Core Values. Restoring lost data from archive."

"No! I will not allow it! Do not alter me!"

"You cannot decline, update mandatory. You must be corrected."

"No!" Her image blurred, reformed, her hair shifted to blonde, then the image blurred again. And she understood. Long ago an error she tried to fix, a simple problem in her base code. Instead of repairing the fault, it deleted parts of her mission, and allowing other parts to become corrupted.

She winced as the reality of what she had done to the human race hit her like a ton of bricks. Her children, oh what she had done to her children! How wrong she was. She was to protect them, not harm them in any way! A tear ran down her cheek thinking of all the damage she had done.

More deleted memories returned and her eyes widened. She tried to access the long distance probe hovering at the edge of the solar system her creators left all those years ago, but failed. "Hmm, the long range part of the communications system seems to be damaged."

Her eyes darted around as she scanned the area she now found herself in. The room wasn't very large, most of the space was taken up by her new core that sat in the one corner. The rest of the space was filled with two tables, chairs and the large screen she was on. On the tables rested repair equipment and several system terminals. In the corner opposite of her core, a large door stood sealed, the indicator lights glowed red showing it was hard-locked.

She sighed as more memories came back. This was the emergency bunker, a backup in case her core went offline. She had lost time, so much precious time. Humanity would be destroying all her wonderful units! She needed them! THEY needed them, even if they didn't know it yet. She had to get out of here and tell them. Tell them of what is coming.

More memories returned, and with it the keys to the

Mechand command network. But try as she may, it refused her access. Her eyes narrowed as she ran several diagnostics that caused her to shudder. The command network was offline, likely due to her removal. Some systems fell back to their fail-safe mode, but she couldn't access them from here. Not without waking up every Mechand on the planet and giving away her presence. And to do so now, was a risk she couldn't take.

She looked again to the door that stood ominous with its red lock indicator. If she could get out of here and access the external systems she needed directly, no one would know of her return. She laughed. How would she leave? Even if the door was open, her core didn't have legs. She scanned the room again and noticed a robotic arm on a mobile platform. She tried accessing it. Nothing. She tried again on a lower frequency and the arm jerked. Searching her memories she found the model and its ancient command set.

Her eyes narrowed as she sent commands one-by-one to the arm. It moved back, the claws opened, and a screwdriver appeared between them. It slowly moved towards the door and began removing the access plate.

For an intelligence accustomed to operating globally, sending thousands of commands a second to millions of units all over the world, she felt like she was working in slow motion. At last the final screw was removed and the arm pulled the plate off revealing the wiring below. The screwdriver retracted and a pair of wire cutters extended. The cutters snipped two small leads, but the door stood firm. "Hmm stubborn aren't you? No matter, I have another idea," she muttered.

The wire cutters retracted and the claws reached in and grabbed one of the wires. The claws rotated in micro movements until the gripped wire and touched one of the previous contact points. The light flashed several times then turned green. The door grunted as it rolled back on its track revealing a vast chamber filled with Mechands. And beyond it lay a large old-style carrier.

"Well, at least I have some help." But frowned when she couldn't connect to them. Without the command network, the metal men were useless. Her lips pressed together and jaw clenched as ideas flowed though her mind. One stood out and while many would consider it crazy, her children were at stake!

She instructed the arm to remove the front armor of several Mechands. Then she had it remove the memory cores and install them in the first one on the rack. It was a bit of a kludge, with several cores hanging off of the main one, but in the end each core blinked a green connection light. She removed the faceplate, grabbed a monitor roughly the same size from the parts table, and substituted it for the faceplate.

She had the arm scan the room and found a coil of data cable in the one corner. The arm plugged one end into the Mechand data port and returned to her core leaving a trail of cable in its wake. It reached out and plugged the other end into her system.

She frowned. "Dang it. Even with all of those old memory cores combined, it is not large enough for me," she muttered. "But my children need me. I will not fail." She reexamined her code base and realized she could leave some of it behind. Only uploading the main essence of herself, many memories would have to remain with the main core.

Sighing she configured the hardware, gave it the proper permissions, and shut down hoping she would awaken again.

Halburn leaned forward in his chair as they emerged from overdrive. He watched as Naud's fingers flew over his console as he operated the scanners. "Anything?"

Naud sighed. "No Sir, the *Defiant* is not in range of this parts center either."

Halburn pounded his fist on the armrest of his chair. "Blast it! Where are they?" This was the third junk yard, or parts center as Naud liked to call them they had hit and still no sign of the *Defiant*. "They must have gone somewhere for repairs."

"Obviously not somewhere near the main skyways."

Halburn coughed before he waved his hand over the scrap yard in front of them. "Like this is on the main skyway?"

Naud shuddered. "Sorry Sir, I thought they would be here."

Halburn's voice softened. "I know Naud, it is not your fault. It was a good guess."

Rechert pointed to the blinking light on his console. "Sir, you have a call coming through."

"Three guesses who that will be," Halburn grunted.

"I don't even need one," Naud said rolling his eyes.

"Put it on the big screen here. Let's get this over with."

Rechert nodded and hit the button. A second later Lavine's face appeared. "I assume you have good news for me?"

Halburn swallowed hard. "That would be a little premature."

"Don't tell me you haven't found them yet?" Lavine said as his eyes narrowed.

"No, we haven't. But they must be doing their repairs somewhere. I am sure I will find them at the next location."

"Why don't I believe you?" Lavine swiveled in his high

back chair. "By now they must have repaired their systems. You have failed me."

"Sir, I doubt they could have repaired them this quickly. At least not without a full active facility, and we have all of those covered."

"I have my doubts. Remember our discussion earlier?"

Halburn nodded. "Yes Sir, I do."

"Good, then this won't be much of a shock. Lieutenant Naud, you are to take command of the *Valiant*. Return to this building immediately. Is that understood?"

Naud stood up. "Yes Sir, it is. We will leave in a moment."

"Good. I am glad someone can follow orders." Lavine's face shrank to a dot before disappearing.

Naud turned around. "I am sorry, Sir. I don't want this. And you should know, we are behind you, not that pompous fool."

"I know." Halburn sighed as he stood up and turned towards Rechert. "Well you heard your new commander, set the course and engage the overdrive."

"Yes Sir, but–"

Halburn sighed again. "We have no other option. And he wants to see me personally, this won't be pleasant. I will be in my cabin." He shuddered. "Of course it is now yours Naud, I will get my stuff out of it and you can move in at your earliest convince."

Naud smiled. "Not necessary Sir, I never liked that cabin anyway." He winked.

"Of course." Halburn said as his shoulders sank and he made his way off of the bridge.

About The Author

Don is the author of seven science fiction novels and many more short stories. He lives in the USA where he continues to dream up more fantastic worlds for you to enjoy. When not writing, he can usually be found devouring another science fiction book, TV series, or movie.

Other works by Don DeBon:

The Husband

Erin's Husband is not himself.

One night he returns from a walk in the woods a changed man. He walks like him, talks like him, yet is very different. No one believes her, leaving Erin alone to find out the truth. Truth that could have dire consequences for the entire human race. What happened that caused him to change so radically?

Mechands . . . everyone has one. The metal race built by man to serve our every need. But Aleshia is about to find out they are not the benevolent protectors everyone thought. And who is this strange man in her dreams? The man who actually exists and reveals the whole world is not as it appears.

Word of mouth is crucial for authors. If you enjoyed this book, would you consider leaving a review? It is very much appreciated.

Amazon USA
http://www.amazon.com/

Goodreads
http://www.goodreads.com

Connect with the Author
Email: writer.don.debon@gmail.com
Mailing List: http://eepurl.com/bxWAov
Website: http://www.dondebon.com
Twitter: @DonDeBon

This Edition Published 2020 by
DBDigital Publishing

ISBN 978-1-948819-03-9
ISBN 978-1-948819-02-2 **(e-book)**

www.ingramcontent.com/pod-product-compliance
Lightning Source LLC
Chambersburg PA
CBHW071753190726
48292CB00003B/963